AF555930

Shri Vishnu Sahasranama Stotram

The One Thousand Names of Vishnu

SANSKRITI PRESS

RUPA

Published in Sanskriti Press
by Rupa Publications India Pvt. Ltd 2024
161-B/4, Gulmohar House,
Yusuf Sarai Community Centre,
New Delhi 110049

Sales centres:
Bengaluru Chennai
Hyderabad Kolkata Mumbai

P-ISBN: 978-93-6156-819-0
E-ISBN: 978-93-6156-828-2

Third impression 2026

10 9 8 7 6 5 4 3

Printed in India

Introduction to the Vishnu Sahasranama

At Rupa Publications, we are proud to bring the profound wisdom of ancient India to the modern reader, and this book on the Vishnu Sahasranama is a testament to that effort. The Vishnu Sahasranama, also known as the Thousand Names of Vishnu, was first chanted in praise of Lord Krishna on the battlefield of Kurukshetra during the Mahabharata, which speaks of a war between two branches of the same family—the Kauravas and the Pandavas. The war, which lasted 18 days, saw immense loss of life, and one of the most notable events was the conversation between Yudhisthira, the eldest of the Pandavas, and the great warrior Bhishma, who lay wounded on a bed of arrows.

Bhishma, who had received the blessing to die only when he wished, remained on the battlefield, awaiting his chosen moment of death. When Yudhisthira and his brothers approached him in deep respect, Bhishma, true to his Dharma, spoke with reverence about their victory. He acknowledged that their success was not solely due to their skills but also because they had the support of the Supreme Lord, Lord Krishna, who was none other than Vishnu Himself. This moment, where Bhishma praised Krishna, is when the Vishnu Sahasranama originates.

On his deathbed, Yudhisthira asked Bhishma profound questions: Who is the greatest Divinity? Who is the one refuge for all? By chanting whose name could one overcome the limitations of Samsara, the endless cycle of birth and death? Bhishma answered these questions by reciting the thousand names of Vishnu, the all-pervading Supreme Being, the essence of the universe, and the master of all worlds. He assured Yudhisthira and his brothers that by chanting these names, mankind could free itself from sorrow and attain the highest spiritual state.

The Vishnu Sahasranama holds immense power. It is believed that chanting these thousand names of Vishnu brings immense benefits, even if the full meaning is not known. Chanting or listening to the Sahasranama can help overcome negative planetary influences, promote spiritual growth, remove financial difficulties, and relieve stress. Furthermore, it is said to create a protective shield around the mind and body, bring peace to the home, and cure physical ailments such as infertility. The transformative power of the Sahasranama extends to removing sins from past lives and propelling us closer to the Supreme Being, Vishnu, ultimately leading to Moksha—salvation and liberation from the cycle of life and death.

Bhishma's teachings have been passed down through generations, and the Vishnu Sahasranama has been chanted in temples and homes for centuries. Today, anyone can experience its divine effects by simply chanting or listening with devotion. The thousand names of Vishnu remind us of His omnipresence and omnipotence, and the benefits of this practice continue to guide and support countless devotees on their spiritual journey.

As we present this book to you, we hope to carry forward this timeless legacy of wisdom, offering you a way to access the profound teachings of the Vishnu Sahasranama. Through the recitation of these sacred names, may you find peace, protection, spiritual growth and the blessings of Lord Vishnu. We hope this book becomes your guide to understanding the ancient knowledge embedded in these powerful chants, helping you connect with the divine and attain spiritual liberation.

Meditation on Vishnu

शुक्लाम्बरधरं विष्णुं
शशिवर्णं चतुर्भुजम् ।
प्रसन्नवदनं ध्यायेत्
सर्वविघ्नोपशान्तये ॥१॥

śuklāṁbaradharaṁ viṣṇuṁ
śaśivarṇaṁ caturbhujam,
prasannavadanaṁ dhyāyet
sarvavighnōpaśāṁtaye. (1)

One should meditate on Vishnu, dressed in white robes, moon-coloured, four-armed, with a cheerful face, for the removal of all obstacles.

यस्य द्विरदवक्त्राद्याः
पारिषद्याः परः शतम् ।
विघ्नं निघ्नन्ति सततं
विष्वक्सेनं तमाश्रये ॥२॥

yasya dviradavaktrādyāḥ
pāriṣadyāḥ paraḥ śatam,
vighnaṁ nighnanti satataṁ
viṣvakasenaṁ tamāśraye. (2)

The Elephant-Faced One, along with His innumerable attendants, would always remove obstacles, as we depend on Vishvaksena.

व्यासं वसिष्ठनप्तारं
शक्तेः पौत्रमकल्मषम् ।
पराशरात्मजं वन्दे
शुकतातं तपोनिधिम् ।।३।।

vyāsaṁ vasiṣṭhanaptāraṁ
śakteḥ pautramakalmaṣam,
parāśarātmajaṁ vaṁde
śukatātaṁ tapōnidhim. (3)

I salute Vyasa, the great-grandson of Vasishta, the grandson of Shakti, the immaculate son of Parasara, the father of Shukata, the treasure of austerities.

व्यासाय विष्णुरूपाय
व्यासरूपाय विष्णवे ।
नमो वै ब्रह्मनिधये
वासिष्ठाय नमो नमः ।।४।।

vyāsāya viṣṇurūpāya
vyāsarūpāya viṣṇave,
namō vai brahmanidhaye
vāsiṣṭhāya namō namaḥ. (4)

O Vyasa in the form of Vishnu, O Vishnu in the form of Vyasa, O Vasishta, the treasure of the Brahman, I offer my obeisances unto Thee again and again.

अविकाराय शुद्धाय
नित्याय परमात्मने ।
सदैकरूपरूपाय
विष्णवे सर्वजिष्णवे ।।५।।

avikārāya śuddhāya
nityāya paramātmane,
sadaikarūparūpāya
viṣṇave sarvajiṣṇave. (5)

Bow I before Vishnu, Who is pure, Who is not affected, Who is permanent, Who is the ultimate truth, and Who wins over all the mortals in this world.

यस्य स्मरणमात्रेण
जन्मसंसारबन्धनात् ।
विमुच्यते नमस्तस्मै
विष्णवे प्रभविष्णवे ।।६।।

yasya smaraṇamātreṇa
janmasaṁsārabaṁdhanāt,
vimucyate namastasmai
viṣṇave prabhaviṣṇave. (6)

Obeisance to that Vishnu, the all-powerful Vishnu, Whose remembrance alone frees one from the bondage of birth and death.

ॐ नमो विष्णवे प्रभविष्णवे ।

– श्रीवैशम्पायन उवाच –

श्रुत्वा धर्मानशेषेण
पावनानि च सर्वशः ।
युधिष्ठिरः शान्तनवं
पुनरेवाभ्यभाषत ।।७।।

oṃ namo viṣṇave prabhaviṣṇave.

- śrī vaiśaṁpāyana uvāca -

śrutvā dharmānaśeṣeṇa
pāvanāni ca sarvaśaḥ,
yudhiṣṭhiraḥ śāṁtanavaṁ
punarevābhyabhyāṣata. (7)

- Shri Vaisampayana said -

Having heard the Dharma in its entirety and the holy ones in all respects, Yudhisthira again addressed Shantanu.

- युधिष्ठिर उवाच -

किमेकं दैवतं लोके किं
वाप्येकं परायणम् ।
स्तुवन्तः कं कमर्चन्तः
प्राप्नुयुर्मानवाः शुभम् ॥८॥

- śrī yudhiṣṭhira uvāca -

kimekaṁ daivataṁ lōke kiṁ
vāpyekaṁ parāyaṇaṁ,
stuvaṁtaḥ kaṁ kamarcaṁtaḥ
prāpnuyurmānavāḥ śubham. (8)

- Yudhisthira asked -

Is there one god in this world, or is there one devotee? Whom do men attain to good by praising and worshipping?

को धर्मः सर्वधर्माणां
भवतः परमो मतः ।
किं जपन्मुच्यते
जन्तुर्जन्मसंसारबन्धनात् ॥९॥

kō dharmaḥ sarvadharmāṇāṁ
bhavataḥ paramō mataḥ,
kiṁ japanmucyate
jaṁturjanmasaṁsārabaṁdhanāt. (9)

Which Dharma do you consider to be the supreme of all Dharma? By chanting what is a creature freed from the bondage of birth and death?

- भीष्म उवाच -

जगत्प्रभुं देवदेवमनन्तं
पुरुषोत्तमम् ।
स्तुवन् नामसहस्रेण
पुरुषः सततोत्थितः ।।१०।।

- śrī bhīṣma uvāca -

jagatprabhuṁ devadevamanaṁtaṁ
puruṣōttamam,
stuvannāmasahasreṇa
puruṣaḥ satatōtthitaḥ. (10)

- Bhishma replied -

Praising the Lord of the Universe, the God of Gods, the infinite Supreme Personality of Godhead, with a thousand names, the man ever rises.

तमेव चार्चयन्नित्यं
भक्त्या पुरुषमव्ययम् ।
ध्यायन् स्तुवन् नमस्यंश्च
यजमानस्तमेव च ।।११।।

tameva cārcayannityaṁ
bhaktyā puruṣamavyayam,
dhyāyan stuvannamasyaṁśca
yajamānastameva ca. (11)

And worshipping Him alone with devotion, meditating on the inexhaustible Purusha, praising and bowing down to Him alone, and offering sacrifices to Him alone, the worshipper, the aspirant (is freed).

अनादिनिधनं विष्णुं
सर्वलोकमहेश्वरम् ।
लोकाध्यक्षं स्तुवन्नित्यं
सर्वदुःखातिगो भवेत ।।१२।।

anādinidhanaṃ viṣṇuṃ
sarvalokamaheśvaram,
lokādhyakṣaṃ stuvannityaṃ
sarvaduḥkhātigo bhavet. (12)

By praising Vishnu, the eternally immortal, the Great Lord of all the worlds, the Presiding Deity of the worlds, one can pass beyond all sorrows.

ब्रह्मण्यं सर्वधर्मज्ञं
लोकानां कीर्तिवर्धनम् ।
लोकनाथं महद्भूतं
सर्वभूतभवोद्भवम् ॥१३॥

brahmaṇyaṁ sarvadharmajñaṁ
lōkānāṁ kīrtivardhanam,
lōkanāthaṁ mahadbhūtaṁ
sarvabhūtabhavōdhbhavam. (13)

He is the Brahman, the Knower of all religions, the Enhancer of the fame of the worlds, the Lord of the worlds, the Great Being, the origin of all beings.

एष मे सर्वधर्माणां
धर्मोऽधिकतमो मतः ।
यद्भक्त्या पुण्डरीकाक्षं
स्तवैरर्चेन्नरः सदा ॥१४॥

eṣa me sarvadharmāṇāṁ
dharmōdhikatamō mataḥ,
yadbhaktyā puṁḍarīkākṣaṁ
stavairarcennaraḥ sadā. (14)

This is the Dharma that I consider to be the highest of all Dharma, that one should always worship the lotus-eyed Lord with devotion and hymns.

परमं यो महत्तेजः
परमं यो महत्तपः ।
परमं यो महद्ब्रह्म
परमं यः परायणम् ।।१५।।

paramaṁ yō mahattejaḥ
paramaṁ yō mahattapaḥ,
paramaṁ yō mahadbrahma
paramaṁ yaḥ parāyaṇam. (15)

He is the supreme great light, He is the supreme great ruler, He is the supreme great Brahman (Absolute), He is the supreme highest goal.

पवित्राणां पवित्रं यो
मङ्गलानां च मङ्गलम् ।
दैवतं दैवतानां च
भूतानां योऽव्ययः पिता ।।१६।।

pavitrāṇāṁ pavitraṁ yō
maṁgalānāṁ ca maṁgalam,
daivataṃ daivatānāṃ ca
bhūtānāṃ yo'vyayaḥ pita. (16)

He Who is holy among the holy and auspicious among the auspicious, Who is God among the gods and Who is the inexhaustible Father of all beings.

यतः सर्वाणि भूतानि
भवन्त्यादियुगागमे ।
यस्मिंश्च प्रलयं यान्ति
पुनरेव युगक्षये ।।१७।।

yataḥ sarvāṇi bhūtāni
bhavaṁtyādiyugāgame,
yasmiṁśca pralayaṁ yāṁti
punareva yugakṣaye. (17)

From Him all creatures proceed in the beginning of an age, and in Him they are absorbed again at the end of the age.

तस्य लोकप्रधानस्य
जगन्नाथस्य भूपते ।
विष्णोर्नामसहस्रं मे
शृणु पापभयापहम् ॥१८॥

tasya lōkapradhānasya
jagannāthasya bhūpate,
viṣṇōrnāmasahasraṁ me
śruṇu pāpabhayāpaham. (18)

Of that Chief of the World, of the Lord of the Universe, O King (Yudhisthira), of Vishnu, hear from me the thousand names, which remove all sin and fear.

यानि नामानि गौणानि
विख्यातानि महात्मनः ।
ऋषिभिः परिगीतानि तानि
वक्ष्यामि भूतये ।।१९।।

yāni nāmāni gauṇāni
vikhyātāni mahātmanaḥ,
ṛṣibhiḥ parigītāni tāni
vakṣyāmi bhūtaye. (19)

Those famous names of the Great Soul, which bring out His manifold qualities celebrated by rishis, I shall declare for the good (of all).

ऋषिर्नाम्नां सहस्रस्य
वेदव्यासो महामुनिः
छन्दोऽनुष्टुप् तथा देवो
भगवान् देवकीसुतः ।।२०।।

ṛṣirnāmnāṁ sahasrasya
vedavyāsō mahāmuniḥ,
chaṁdōnuṣṭup tathā devō
bhagavān devakīsutaḥ. (20)

The rishi of the thousand names is Vedavyasa, the great contemplative sage. The metre is Anushtup, and the deity is the blessed son of Devaki.

अमृतांशूद्भवो बीजं
शक्तिर्देवकिनन्दनः ।
त्रिसामा हृदयं तस्य
शान्त्यर्थे विनियोज्यते ।।२१।।

amrtāṁśūdbhavō bījaṁ
śaktirdevakinaṁdana:
trisāmā hrdayaṁ tasya
śāṁtyarthe viniyojyate. (21)

The seed is He-who-was-born-in-the-lunar-race, its power is The Name, The-son-of-Devaki. The heart is the One-who-is-lauded-by-the-three-Sama-hymns, the purpose of its use is the attainment of peace.

विष्णुं जिष्णुं महाविष्णुं
प्रभविष्णुं महेश्वरम्
अनेकरूप दैत्यान्तं
नमामि पुरुषोत्तमम् ।।२२।।

viṣṇuṁ jiṣṇuṁ mahāviṣṇuṁ
prabhaviṣṇuṁ maheśvaram,
anekarūpa daityāṁtaṁ
namāmi puruṣōttamam. (22)

Vishnu, Conqueror, Great Vishnu, Creator, the Great Lord, to Him of many forms, the Destroyer of Demons, to the Supreme Person, I bow.

पूर्वन्यासः

– श्रीवेदव्यास उवाच –

ॐ अस्य श्रीविष्णोर्दिव्यसहस्रनामस्तोत्र
महामन्त्रस्य ।
श्री वेदव्यासो भगवान् ऋषिः ।
अनुष्टुप् छन्दः ।
श्रीमहाविष्णुः परमात्मा श्रीमन्नारायणो देवता ।
अमृतांशूद्भवो भानुरिति बीजम् ।
देवकीनन्दनः स्रष्टेति शक्तिः ।
उद्भवः क्षोभणो देव इति परमो मन्त्रः ।
शङ्खभृन्नन्दकी चक्रीति कीलकम् ।
शार्ङ्गधन्वा गदाधर इत्यस्त्रम् ।
रथाङ्गपाणिरक्षोभ्य इति नेत्रम् ।
त्रिसामा सामगः सामेति कवचम् ।
आनन्दं परब्रह्मेति योनिः ।
ऋतुः सुदर्शनः काल इति दिग्बन्धः ।।
श्रीविश्वरूप इति ध्यानम् ।
श्रीमहाविष्णुप्रीत्यर्थे सहस्रनामस्तोत्रपाठे विनियोगः ।।

pūrvanyāsaḥ

- śrīvedavyāsa uvāca -

oṃ asya śrī viṣṇōrdivyasahasranāmastōtra
mahāmaṁtrasya,
śrī vēdavyāsō bhagavān r̥ṣiḥ,
anuṣṭup chaṁdaḥ,
śrīmahāviṣṇuḥ paramātmā
śrīmannārāyaṇō dēvatā,
amr̥tāṁśūdbhavō bhānuriti bījam,
dēvakīnaṁdanaḥ sraṣṭēti śaktiḥ,
udhbhavaḥ, kṣōbhaṇō dēva iti paramō maṁtraḥ,
śaṁkhabhr̥nnaṁdakī cakrīti kīlakam,
śārṅgadhanvā gadādhara ityastram,
rathāṁgapāṇirakṣōbhya iti nētram,
trisāmā sāmagaḥ sāmēti kavacam,
ānaṁdaṁ parabrahmēti yōniḥ,
r̥tussudarśana: kāla iti digbhaṁdhaḥ,
śrī viśvarūpa iti dhyānam,
śrīmahāviṣṇuprītyarthē sahasranāma
pārāyaṇē viniyōgaḥ.

- Vedavyasa said -

Om; of this garland of mantras (constituting) the praise-song of the divine thousand names of Vishnu,

The blessed Vedavyasa is the seer, Krishna, the Supreme Self, is the deity, the metre is Anushtup,

'Having His source in the Self, Self-Begotten' is the seed,

'The son of Devaka, the Creator and Sustainer' is the Power,

'He whose glory is sung in the three types of Sama songs' is the theme of such songs,

'He who manifests Himself as the Sama Veda' is the heart,

'The Bearer of the conch, He of the word, He of the discus' is the nail, 'He of the Sharnga bow, the Wielder of the mace' is the weapon, 'The One holding the reins of a chariot in His hands (Krishna), who is imperturbable' is the armour,

'The source, the vibration, God' is the supreme mantra.

Let us engage ourselves in the Japa of the divine thousand names of Vishnu for the purpose of pleasing Great Vishnu.

अथ ध्यानम् ।

क्षीरोदन्वत्प्रदेशे
शुचिमणिविलसत्सैकते मौक्तिकानां मालाकॢप्तासनस्थः स्फटिकमणि
निभैर्मौक्तिकैर्मण्डिताङ्गः ।
शुभ्रैरभ्रैरदभ्रैरुपरिविर
चितैर्मुक्तपीयूष वर्षैः
आनन्दी नः पुनीयादरिनलिनगदा
शङ्खपाणिर्मुकुन्दः ॥१॥

atha dhyānam

kṣīrōdanvatpradēśē
śucimaṇivilasatsaikatē mauktikānāṁ
mālāklṛptāsanasthaḥ sphaṭikamaṇi
nibhairmauktikairmaṁ-ḍitāṁgaḥ,
śubhrairabhrairadabhrairuparivira
citairmuktapīyūṣa varṣaiḥ
ānaṁdīnaḥ punīyādarinaḷinagadā
śaṁkhapāṇirmukuṁdaḥ. (1)

In the region of the ocean of milk, seated on a garland of pure gems and pearls, adorned with pearls resembling crystal gems, with white clouds, with rains of free nectar, delighting us, may the lotus and mace of the holy mountains, holding a conch, be our joy.

भूः पादौ यस्य
नाभिर्वियदसुरनिलश्चन्द्र
सूर्यौ च नेत्रे
कर्णावाशाः शिरो द्यौर्मुखमपि
दहनो यस्य वास्तेयमब्धिः ।
अन्तःस्थं यस्य विश्वं
सुरनरखगगोभोगिगन्धर्वदैत्यैः
चित्रं रंरम्यते तं त्रिभुवन
वपुषं विष्णुमीशं नमामि ।।२।।

bhūḥ pādau yasya
nābhirviyadasuranilaścaṁdra
sūryau ca nētrē
karṇāvāśāḥ śirō dyaurmukhamapi
dahanō yasya vāsōyamabdhiḥ,
aṁtaḥsthaṁ yasya viśvaṁ uranarakhagagōbh
ōgigaṁdharvadaityaiḥ,
citraṁ raṁ ramyatē taṁ tribhuvana
vapuṣaṁ viṣṇumīśaṁ namāmi. (2)

I bow before that God, Vishnu, Who is the lord of three worlds, Who has earth as his feet, Who has air as his soul, Who has sky as his belly, Who has moon and sun as eyes, Who has the four directions as ears, Who has the land of gods as head, Who has fire as his mouth, Who has sea as his stomach, And in whose belly play and enjoy, Gods, men birds, animals, Serpent men, Gandharvas and Asuras.

ॐ शान्ताकारं भुजगशयनं
पद्मनाभं सुरेशं
विश्वाधारं गगनसदृशं
मेघवर्णं शुभाङ्गम् ।
लक्ष्मीकान्तं कमलनयनं
योगिहृद्ध्यानगम्यमं
वन्दे विष्णुं भवभयहरं
सर्वलोकैकनाथम् ।।३।।

oṃ śāṁtākāraṁ bhujagaśayanaṁ
padmanābhaṁ surēśaṁ
viśvādhāraṁ gaganasadr̥śaṁ
mēghavarṇaṁ śubhāṁgam,
lakṣmīkāṁtaṁ kamalanayanaṁ
yōgihr̥ddhyānagamyaṁ
vaṁdē viṣṇuṁ bhavabhayaharaṁ
sarvalōkaikanātham. (3)

I bow before God Vishnu, Who is personification of peace, Who sleeps on his folded arms, Who has a lotus on his belly, Who is the God of gods, Who is the basis of earth, Who is like the sky, Who is of the colour of the cloud, Who has beautiful limbs, Who is the consort of Lakshmi, Who has lotus-like eyes, Who is seen by saints through thought, Who kills all worries and fears, and Who is the Lord of all the worlds.

मेघश्यामं पीतकौशेयवासं
श्रीवत्साङ्कं कौस्तुभोद्भासिताङ्गम् ।
पुण्योपेतं पुण्डरीकायताक्षं
विष्णुं वन्दे सर्वलोकैकनाथम् ।।४।।

mēghaśyāmaṁ pītakauśēyavāsaṁ
śrīvatsāṁkaṁ kaustubhōdbhāsitāṁgam,
puṇyōpētaṁ puṁḍarīkāyatākṣaṁ
viṣṇuṁ vaṁdē sarvalōkaikanātham. (4)

I bow before that God Vishnu, Who is the Lord of all the universe, Who is black like a cloud, Who wears yellow silks, Who has the Sreevatsa on him, Whose limbs shine because of Kousthubha, Who has eyes like an open lotus, and Who is surrounded by the blessed always.

नमः समस्तभूतानामादि
भूताय भूभृते ।
अनेकरूपरूपाय
विष्णवे प्रभविष्णवे ।।५।।

namaḥ samastabhūtānāmādi
bhūtāya bhūbhṛte,
anekarūparūpāya
viṣṇave prabhaviṣṇave. (5)

Obeisance to Vishnu, the origin of all beings, the Sustainer of the earth, the form of many forms, the Originator.

सशङ्खचक्रं सकिरीटकुण्डलं
सपीतवस्त्रं सरसीरुहेक्षणम् ।
सहारवक्षःस्थलशोभिकौस्तुभं
नमामि विष्णुं शिरसा चतुर्भुजम् ।।६।।

saśaṁkhacakraṁ sakirīṭakuṁḍalaṁ
sapītavastraṁ sarasīruhēkṣaṇam,
sahāravakṣaḥsthalaśōbhikaustubhaṁ
namāmi viṣṇuṁ śirasā caturbhujam. (6)

I bow before God Vishnu, Who has four arms, Who has a conch and wheel in his hands, Who wears a crown and earrings, Who wears yellow silks, Who has lotus-like eyes, Who shines because of Kousthbha gem worn on his garlanded chest.

छायायां पारिजातस्य हेमसिंहासनोपरि
आसीनमम्बुदश्याममायता क्षमलंकृतम् ।
चन्द्राननं चतुर्बाहुं श्रीवत्साङ्कित वक्षसं
रुक्मिणी सत्यभामाभ्यां सहितं कृष्णमाश्रये ।।७।।

chāyāyāṁ pārijātasya hēmasiṁhāsanōpari
āsīnamaṁbudaśyāmamāyatā kṣamalaṁkr̥tam,
caṁdrānanaṁ caturbāhuṁ
śrīvatsāṁkita vakṣasam
rukmiṇī satyabhāmābhyāṁ
sahitaṁ kr̥ṣṇamāśrayē. (7)

I seek refuge in Lord Krishna, Who is with Rukhmani and Satyabhama, Who sits on a golden throne in the shade of Parijata tree, Who is of the colour of the black cloud, Who has long broad eyes, Who has a face like moon, Who has four hands, and Who has a chest adorned by Sreevatsa.

Stotram 1,000 Names

विश्वं विष्णुर्वषट्कारो भूतभव्यभवत्प्रभुः ।
भूतकृद्भूतभृद्भावो भूतात्मा भूतभावनः ॥१॥

viśvaṁ viṣṇurvaṣaṭkārō
bhūtabhavyabhavatprabhuḥ,
bhūtakṛdbhūtabhṛdbhāvō
bhūtātmā bhūtabhāvanaḥ. (1)

1. **Viśvaṁ:** The all or the Universe.
2. **Viṣṇuḥ:** He who pervades everything.
3. **Vaṣaṭkāraḥ:** For whom the sacrificial versus are uttered in the yajnas.
4. **Bhūta-bhavya-bhavat-prabhuḥ:** One who is the master and beyond the past, present and the future.
5. **Bhūtakṛd:** The creator and destroyer of all existences in the universe.
6. **Būtabhṛd:** One who supports or sustains or governs the universe.
7. **Bhāvaḥ:** Pure existence.
8. **Bhūtātmā:** The essence of all beings.
9. **Bhūta-bhāvanaḥ:** He who originates and develops all elements.

पूतात्मा परमात्मा च मुक्तानां परमा गतिः ।
अव्ययः पुरुषः साक्षी क्षेत्रज्ञोऽक्षर एव च ॥२॥

pūtātmā paramātmā ca
muktānāṁ paramā gatiḥ,
avyayaḥ puruṣaḥ sākṣī
kṣetrajñōkṣara eva ca. (2)

10. **Pūtātmā:** One whose nature is purity/who is purity.
11. **Paramātmā:** He who is the supreme one and the Atman.
12. **Muktānāṁ paramā gatiḥ:** The highest goal of the liberated ones.
13. **Avyayaḥ:** One for whom there is no decay.
14. **Puruṣaḥ:** One who abides in the body or pura.
15. **Sākṣī:** One who witnesses everything.
16. **Kṣetrajñaḥ:** The knower of the field or body.
17. **Akṣara:** He who is without destruction.

योगो योगविदां नेता प्रधानपुरुषेश्वरः ।
नारसिंहवपुः श्रीमान् केशवः पुरुषोत्तमः ।।३।।

yōgō yōgavidāṁ netā
pradhānapuruṣeśvaraḥ,
nārasiṁhavapuḥ śrīmān
keśavaḥ puruṣōttamaḥ. (3)

18. **Yogaḥ:** One attainable through Yoga.
19. **Yogavidāṁ netā:** The master of those who are established in the above-mentioned Yoga.
20. **Pradhāna-puruṣeśvaraḥ:** The master of Pradhana or Prakriti and Purusha or Jiva.
21. **Nārasiṁha-vapuḥ:** One in whom the bodies of a man and a lion are combined.
22. **Śrimān:** One on whose chest Goddess Shri always dwells.
23. **Keśavaḥ:** One whose Kesa or locks are beautiful.
24. **Puruṣottamaḥ:** The greatest among all Purushas.

सर्वः शर्वः शिवः
स्थाणुर्भूतादिर्निधिरव्ययः ।
सम्भवो भावनो भर्ता
प्रभवः प्रभुरीश्वरः ॥४॥

sarvaḥ śarvaḥ śivaḥ
sthāṇurbhūtādirnidhiravyayaḥ,
saṁbhavō bhāvanō bhartā
prabhavaḥ prabhurīśvaraḥ. (4)

25. **Sarvaḥ:** The omniscient source of all existence.
26. **Śarvaḥ:** Destroyer.
27. **Śivaḥ:** One pure.
28. **Sthāṇur:** One who is steady, immovable and changeless.
29. **Bhūtādiḥ:** Source of all elements or existing things.
30. **Nidhir-avyayaḥ:** The changeless and indestructible Being in whom the whole universe becomes merged and remains in seminal condition at the time of Pralaya or cosmic dissolution.

31. **Sambhavaḥ:** One born out of His own will as incarnation.
32. **Bhāvanaḥ:** One who generates the fruits or Karmas (work) of all Jivas for them to enjoy.
33. **Bhartā:** One who supports the universe as its substratum.
34. **Prabhavaḥ:** One from whom all the great elements have their birth or One who has exalted births as incarnations.
35. **Prabhuḥ:** One who is an adept in all rites.
36. **Iśvaraḥ:** One who has unlimited lordliness or power over all things.

स्वयम्भूः शम्भुरादित्यः
पुष्कराक्षो महास्वनः ।
अनादिनिधनो धाता
विधाता धातुरुत्तमः ॥५॥

svayaṁbhūḥ śaṁbhurādityaḥ
puṣkarākṣō mahāsvanaḥ,
anādinidhanō dhātā
vidhātā dhāturuttamaḥ. (5)

37. **Svayambhūḥ:** One who exists by Himself, uncaused by any other.

38. **Śaṁbhuḥ:** One who bestows happiness on devotees.

39. **Ādityaḥ:** The golden-hued person in the sun's orb.

40. **Puṣkarākṣaḥ:** One who has eyes resembling the petals of Pushkara or lotus.

41. **Mahāsvanaḥ:** One from whom comes the great sound—the Veda.

42. **Anāndi-nidhanaḥ:** The one existence that has neither birth nor death.

43. **Dhātā:** One who is the support of the universe.

44. **Vidhātā:** He who generates Karmas and their fruits.

45. **Dhāturuttamaḥ:** The ultimate support of every thing.

अप्रमेयो हृषीकेशः
पद्मनाभोऽमरप्रभुः ।
विश्वकर्मा मनुस्त्वष्टा
स्थविष्ठः स्थविरो ध्रुवः ॥६॥

aprameyō hṛṣīkeśaḥ
padmanābho'maraprabhuḥ,
viśvakarmā manusvtaṣṭā
sthaviṣṭhaḥ sthaviro dhruvaḥ. (6)

46. **Aprameyaḥ:** One who is not measurable or understandable by any of the accepted means of knowledge like sense, perception, inference, etc.

47. **Hṛṣīkeśaḥ:** The master of the senses or He under whose control the senses subsist.

48. **Padmanābhaḥ:** He in whose navel (nabhi) the lotus (padma), the source of the universe, stands.

49. **Amara-prabhuḥ:** The master of Amaras or the deathless ones, i.e., the Devas.

50. **Viśvakarmā:** He whose Karma has resulted in Vishvam (all that exists) or He whose power of creation is unique and wonderful.

51. **Manuḥ:** He who thinks.

52. **Tvaṣṭā:** He who makes all beings shrunken (Tanukarana) at the time of cosmic dissolution.

53. **Sthaviṣṭaḥ:** He who excels in everything in bulk or substantiality.

54. **Sthaviraḥ-dhruvaḥ:** The Eternal One, being the most ancient. It is taken as a single phrase, the name along with its qualification.

अग्राह्यः शाश्वतः कृष्णो
लोहिताक्षः प्रतर्दनः ।
प्रभूतस्त्रिककुब्धाम
पवित्रं मङ्गलं परम् ।।७।।

agrāhyaḥ śāśvataḥ kṛṣṇō
lōhitākṣaḥ pratardanaḥ,
prabhūtastrikakubdhāma
pavitraṁ maṁgalaṁ param. (7)

55. **Agrāhyaḥ:** One who cannot be grasped by the organs or knowledge or conceived by the mind.

56. **Śāśvataḥ:** One who exists at all times.

57. **Kṛṣṇaḥ:** The existence-Knowledge-Bliss.

58. **Lohitākṣaḥ:** One whose eyes are tinged red.

59. **Pratardanaḥ:** Destroyer of all at the time of cosmic dissolution.

60. **Prabhūtaḥ:** Great because of unique qualities like omnipotence, omniscience, etc.

61. **Tri-kakub-dhāma:** He who is the support (Dharma) of the three regions above, below and in the middle.

62. **Pavitraṁ:** That which purifies everything.

63. **Maṅgalaṁ param:** Supremely auspicious.

ईशानः प्राणदः प्राणो
ज्येष्ठः श्रेष्ठः प्रजापतिः ।
हिरण्यगर्भो भूगर्भो
माधवो मधुसूदनः ॥८॥

Īśānaḥ prāṇadaḥ prāṇō
jyeṣṭhaḥ śreṣṭhaḥ prajāpatiḥ,
hiraṇyagarbhō bhūgarbhō
mādhavō madhusūdanaḥ. (8)

64. **Īśānaḥ:** He who controls and regulates everything.
65. **Prāṇadaḥ:** One who bestows or activates the Prana, the vital energy.
66. **Prāṇaḥ:** The Supreme Being.
67. **Jyeṣṭhaḥ:** The eldest of all, for there is nothing before Him.
68. **Śreṣṭhaḥ:** One deserving the highest praise.
69. **Prajāpatiḥ:** The master of all living beings, because He is Ishvara.
70. **Hiraṇyagarbhaḥ:** One who is Atman of even Brahma the creator.

71. **Bhūgarbhaḥ:** One who has got the world within Himself.

72. **Mādhavaḥ:** The Consort of Ma or Mahalakshmi or One who is fit to be known through Madhu-Vidya.

73. **Madhusūdanaḥ:** The destroyer of the demon Madhu.

ईश्वरो विक्रमी धन्वी
मेधावी विक्रमः क्रमः ।
अनुत्तमो दुराधर्षः
कृतज्ञः कृतिरात्मवान् ॥९॥

Īśvarō vikramī dhanvī
medhāvī vikramaḥ kramaḥ,
anuttamō durādharṣaḥ
kṛtajñaḥ kṛtirātmavān. (9)

74. **Īśvaraḥ:** The omnipotent being.
75. **Vikramī:** The courageous one.
76. **Dhanvī:** One armed with bow.
77. **Medhāvī:** He who has great intelligence capable of grasping all texts.
78. **Vikramaḥ:** He who crosses (Karmana), i.e., transcends Samsara or One who has Vih (bird, i.e., Garuda) as His mount.
79. **Kramaḥ:** Vishnu is called Kramah because He is the cause of Kramana or crossing of the ocean of Samsara by devotees, or because from Him all Krama or manifestation of the universe, has taken place.

80. **Anuttamaḥ:** He than whom there is none greater.

81. **Durādharṣaḥ:** One whom none (Asuras) can overcome.

82. **Kṛtajñaḥ:** One who knows everything about what has been done (Kruta) by Jivas. Also One who is pleased even with those who offer such simple offerings as leaves, flowers, fruits and water.

83. **Kṛtiḥ:** The word means something that is achieved through efforts.

84. **Ātmavān:** One established in his own greatness, i.e., requiring no other support than Himself.

सुरेशः शरणं शर्म
विश्वरेताः प्रजाभवः ।
अहः संवत्सरो व्यालः
प्रत्ययः सर्वदर्शनः ॥१०॥

sureśaḥ śaraṇaṁ śarma
viśvaretāḥ prajābhavaḥ,
ahaḥ saṁvatsarō vyālaḥ
pratyayassarvadarśanaḥ. (10)

85. **Sureśaḥ:** The lord of the Suras or Devas. It can also mean the greatest of those who bestow good.

86. **Śaraṇaṁ:** One who removes the sorrows of those in distress.

87. **Śarma:** One who is of the nature of supreme bliss.

88. **Viśvaretāḥ:** The seed of the universe.

89. **Prajābhavaḥ:** He from whom all beings have originated.

90. **Ahaḥ:** The luminous one.

91. **Saṁvasaraḥ:** As Time is a form of Vishnu, He is called Samvasara or a year.

92. **Vyālaḥ:** One who is ungraspable like a serpent.

93. **Pratyayaḥ:** One who is of the nature of Pratiti or Prajna (consciousness).

94. **Sarva-darśanaḥ:** One with eyes everywhere. As the Lord has assumed all forms, the eyesight of all beings is His.

अजः सर्वेश्वरः सिद्धः
सिद्धिः सर्वादिरच्युतः ।
वृषाकपिरमेयात्मा
सर्वयोगविनिःसृतः ॥११॥

ajaḥ sarveśvaraḥ siddhaḥ
siddhiḥ sarvādiracyutaḥ,
vṛṣākapirameyātmā
sarvayōgaviniḥsṛtaḥ. (11)

95. **Ajah:** One who has no birth.
96. **Sarveśvaraḥ:** The Lord of all lords or the supreme Lord.
97. **Siddhaḥ:** One ever established in one's own nature.
98. **Siddhiḥ:** One who is of the nature of consciousness in all.
99. **Sarvādiḥ:** One who is the first cause of all elements.
100. **Achyutaḥ:** One who never lost and will never lose his inherent nature and powers.
101. **Vṛṣākapiḥ:** One who dispels all suffering and rewards all desires by simply being remembered.

102. **Ameyātmā:** One whose form or nature cannot be measured and determined.

103. **Sarvayoga-viniḥsṛutaḥ:** One who stands aside completely from all bondage.

वसुर्वसुमनाः सत्यः
समात्माऽसम्मितः समः ।
अमोघः पुण्डरीकाक्षो
वृषकर्मा वृषाकृतिः ।।१२।।

vasurvasumanāḥ satyaḥ
samātmā sammitaḥ samaḥ,
amōghaḥ puṇḍarīkākṣō
vṛṣakarmā vṛṣākṛtiḥ. (12)

104. **Vasuḥ:** One in whom all beings dwell and One who dwells in all beings.

105. **Vasumanāḥ:** One who possesses a great mind, i.e., a mind free from attachments, anger and other evil qualities.

106. **Satyaḥ:** One whose nature is Truth.

107. **Samātmā:** One whose mind is Sama, without partiality or anger and thus the same towards all beings.

108. **Sammitaḥ:** 'Sammitah' means measured. He is measurable by His devotees alone.

109. **Samaḥ:** One unpertubed at all times.

110. **Amoghaḥ:** One whose worship will never go in vain, but will bear ample fruits.

111. **Puṇḍarīkākṣaḥ:** One who has pervaded, i.e., is realized in, the lotus of the heart or One whose eyes resemble the petals of a lotus.

112. **Vṛṣakarmā:** One whose actions are according to Vrushas, i.e., Dharma.

113. **Vṛṣāakṛtiḥ:** One who takes form for the sake of Vrushas or Dharma.

रुद्रो बहुशिरा
बभ्रुर्विश्वयोनिः शुचिश्रवाः ।
अमृतः शाश्वत
स्थाणुर्वरारोहो महातपाः ।।१३।।

rudrō bahuśirā
babhrurviśvayōniḥ śuciśravāḥ,
amṛtaḥ śāśvataḥ
sthāṇurvarārōhō mahātapāḥ. (13)

114. **Rudraḥ:** One who makes all beings cry at the time of cosmic dissolution.
115. **Bahuśirāḥ:** One with innumerable heads.
116. **Babhruḥ:** One who governs the world.
117. **Viśvayoniḥ:** One who is the cause of the world.
118. **Śuciśravāḥ:** One whose names and glories are very holy and purifying to be heard.
119. **Amṛtaḥ:** One who is deathless.
120. **Śāśvata-sthāṇuḥ:** One who is both eternal and firmly established, unchanging.
121. **Varārohaḥ:** He whose lap gives the highest blessings.

122. **Mahātapāḥ:** The austerity connected with creation, which is of the nature of knowledge is of great potency.

सर्वगः सर्वविद्भानुर्विष्वक्सेनो
जनार्दनः ।
वेदो वेदविदव्यङ्गो
वेदाङ्गो वेदवित् कविः ।।१४।।

sarvagaḥ sarvavidbhānurviṣvaksenō
janārdanaḥ,
vedō vedavidavyaṅgō
vedāṅgō vedavit kaviḥ. (14)

123. **Sarvagaḥ:** One who pervades everything, being of the nature of their material cause.

124. **Sarvavid-bhānuḥ:** One who is omniscient and illumines everything.

125. **Viṣvakśenaḥ:** He before whom all Asura armies get scattered.

126. **Janārdanaḥ:** One who inflicts suffering on evil men.

127. **Vedaḥ:** He who is of the form of the Veda.

128. **Vedavid:** One who knows the Veda and its meaning.

129. **Avyaṅgaḥ:** One who is self-fulfilled by knowledge and other great attributes and is free from every defect.

130. **Vedāṅgaḥ:** He to whom the Vedas stand as organs.

131. **Vedavit:** One who knows all the Vedas.

132. **Kaviḥ:** One who sees everything.

लोकाध्यक्षः सुराध्यक्षो
धर्माध्यक्षः कृताकृतः ।
चतुरात्मा
चतुर्व्यूहश्चतुर्दंष्ट्रश्चतुर्भुजः ॥१५॥

lōkādhyakṣaḥ surādhyakṣō
dharmādhyakṣaḥ kṛtākṛta:
caturātmā
caturvyūhaścaturdaṁṣṭraścaturbhujaḥ. (15)

133. **Lokādhyakṣaḥ:** He who witnesses the whole universe.

134. **Surākādhyakṣaḥ:** One who is the overlord of the protecting divinities of all regions.

135. **Dharmādhyakṣaḥ:** One who directly sees the merits (Dharma) and demerits (Adharma) of beings by bestwing their due rewards on all beings.

136. **Kṛtākṛtaḥ:** One who is an effect in the form of the worlds and also a non-effect as their cause.

137. **Caturātmā:** One who for the sake of creation, sustenance and dissolution assumes forms.

138. **Chaturvyūhaḥ:** One who adopts a fourfold manifestation.

139. **Chatur-daṁṣṭraḥ:** One with four fangs in His Incarnation as Nisimha.

140. **Chatur-bhujaḥ:** One with four arms.

भ्राजिष्णुर्भोजनं भोक्ता
सहिष्णुर्जगदादिजः ।
अनघो विजयो जेता
विश्वयोनिः पुनर्वसुः ।।१६।।

bhrājiṣṇurbhōjanaṁ bhōktā
sahiṣṇurjagadādijaḥ,
anaghō vijayō jetā
viśvayōniḥ punarvasuḥ. (16)

141. **Bhrājiṣṇuḥ:** One who is pure luminosity.
142. **Bhojanam:** Meal that is enjoyed by the Lord.
143. **Bhoktā:** As he, Purusha, enjoys the Prakruti, He is called the enjoyer or Bhokta.
144. **Sahiṣṇuḥ:** One who forgives.
145. **Jagadādhijaḥ:** One who manifested as Hiranyagarbha by Himself at the beginning of creation.
146. **Anaghaḥ:** The sinless one.
147. **Vijayaḥ:** One who has mastery over the whole universe by virtue of his six special excellences like omnipotence, omniscience etc. known as Bhagas.

148. **Jetā:** One who is naturally victorious over beings, i.e., superior to all beings.

149. **Viśvayoniḥ:** The source of the universe.

150. **Punarvasuḥ:** One who dwells again and again in the bodies as the Jivas.

उपेन्द्रो वामनः
प्रांशुरमोघः शुचिरूर्जितः ।
अतीन्द्रः सङ्ग्रहः सर्गो
धृतात्मा नियमो यमः ।।१७।।

upendrō vāmanaḥ
prāṁśuramōghaḥ śucirūrjitaḥ.
atīndraḥ saṅgrahaḥ sargō
dhṛtātmā niyamō yama. (17)

151. **Upendraḥ:** One born as the younger brother of Indra.
152. **Vāmanaḥ:** One who, in the form of Vamana (dwarf), went begging to Bali.
153. **Prāṁśuḥ:** One of great height.
154. **Amoghaḥ:** One whose acts do not go in vain.
155. **Śuchiḥ:** One who purifies those who adore and praise Him.
156. **Ūrjitaḥ:** One of infinite strength.
157. **Atīndraḥ:** One who is superior to Indra by His inherent attributes like omnipotence, omniscience, etc.

158. **Saṅgrahaḥ:** One who is of the subtle form of the universe to be created.

159. **Sargaḥ:** The creator of Himself.

160. **Dhṛtātmā:** One who is ever in His inherent form or nature, without the transformation involved in birth and death.

161. **Niyamaḥ:** One who appoints His creatures in particular stations.

162. **Yamaḥ:** One who regulates all, remaining within them.

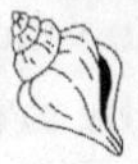

वेद्यो वैद्यः सदायोगी
वीरहा माधवो मधुः ।
अतीन्द्रियो महामायो
महोत्साहो महाबलः ॥१८॥

vedyō vaidyaḥ sadāyōgī
vīrahā mādhavō madhuḥ,
atīndriyō mahāmāyō
mahōtsāhō mahābalaḥ. (18)

163. **Vedyaḥ:** One who has to be known by those who aspire for Moksha.
164. **Vaidhyaḥ:** One who knows all Vidyas or branches of knowledge.
165. **Sadāyogī:** One who is ever experienceble, being ever existent.
166. **Vīrahā:** One who destroys heroic Asuras for the protection of Dharma.
167. **Mādhavaḥ:** One who is the Lord or Master of Ma or knowledge.
168. **Madhuḥ:** Honey because the Lord gives joy, just like honey.

169. **Atīndriyaḥ:** One who is not knowable by the senses.

170. **Mahāmāyaḥ:** One who can cause illusion even over other great illusionists.

171. **Mahotsāhaḥ:** One who is ever busy in the work of creation, sustenance and dissolution.

172. **Mahābalaḥ:** The strongest among all who have strength.

महाबुद्धिर्महावीर्यो
महाशक्तिर्महाद्युतिः ।
अनिर्देश्यवपुः
श्रीमानमेयात्मा महाद्रिधृक् ।।१६।।

mahābuddhirbmahāvīryō
mahāśaktirmahādyutiḥ,
anirdeśyavapuḥ
śrīmānameyātmā mahādridhṛk. (19)

173. **Mahābuddiḥ:** The wisest among the wise.
174. **Mahāvīryaḥ:** The most powerful one.
175. **Mahāśaktiḥ:** One with great resources of strength and skill.
176. **Mahādyutiḥ:** One who is intensely brilliant both within and without.
177. **Anirdeśya-vapuḥ:** One who cannot be indicated to another as: 'He is this', because He cannot be objectively known.
178. **Śrīmān:** One endowed with greatness of every kind.
179. **Ameyātmā:** The Spirit with intelligence that cannot be measured by anyone.

180. **Mahādridhṛk:** One who held up the great mountain Mandara at the time of the churning of the Milk Ocean and also Govardhana in his Krishna incarnation.

महेष्वासो महीभर्ता
श्रीनिवासः सतां गतिः ।
अनिरुद्धः सुरानन्दो
गोविन्दो गोविदां पतिः ॥२०॥

maheṣvāsō mahībhartā
śrīnivāsaḥ satāṁ gatiḥ,
aniruddhaḥ surānandō
gōvindō gōvidāṁ patiḥ. (20)

181. **Maheṣvāsaḥ:** One equipped with the great bow.
182. **Mahībhartā:** One who held up the earth submerged in Pralaya waters.
183. **Śrīnivāsaḥ:** One on whose chest Goddess Shri, eternal in nature, dwells.
184. **Satāṁgatiḥ:** One who bestows the highest destiny attainable, to all holy men.
185. **Aniruddhaḥ:** One who has never been obstructed by anyone or anything from manifesting in various forms.
186. **Surānandaḥ:** One who bestows joy on all divinities.

187. **Govindaḥ:** One who enlivens the cows and the senses.

188. **Govidāṁ patiḥ:** 'Gau' means words. One who knows them is Govid. He who is the master of words is indicated by this name.

मरीचिर्दमनो हंसः
सुपर्णो भुजगोत्तमः ।
हिरण्यनाभः सुतपाः
पद्मनाभः प्रजापतिः ॥२१॥

marīcirdamanō haṁsaḥ
suparṇō bhujagōttamaḥ,
hiraṇyanābhaḥ sutapāḥ
padmanābhaḥ prajāpati (21)

189. **Marīciḥ:** The supreme power and impressiveness seen in persons endowed with such qualities.

190. **Damanaḥ:** One who in the form of Yama inflicts punishments on those who tread the path of unrighteousness.

191. **Haṁsaḥ:** One who removes the fear of Samsara from those who practise the sense of identity with Him.

192. **Suparṇaḥ:** One who has two wings in the shape of Dharma and Adharma.

193. **Bhujagottamaḥ:** One who is the greatest among those who move on Bhujas or arms,

i.e., serpents. The great serpents like Ananta and Vasuki are the powers of Vishnu, so he has come to have this name.

194. **Hiraṇyanābhaḥ:** From whose golden navel arose the lord of creation Brahma.

195. **Sutapāḥ:** One who performs rigorous austerities at Badarikashrama as Nara and Narayana.

196. **Padmanābhaḥ:** One whose navel is beautifully shaped like lotus.

197. **Prajāpatiḥ:** The father of all beings, who are His children.

अमृत्युः सर्वदृक् सिंहः
सन्धाता सन्धिमान् स्थिरः ।
अजो दुर्मर्षणः शास्ता
विश्रुतात्मा सुरारिहा ।।२२।।

amṛtyuḥ sarvadṛk siṁhaḥ
sandhātā sandhimān sthiraḥ,
ajō durmarṣaṇaḥ śāstā
viśrutātmā surārihā. (22)

198. **Amṛtyuḥ:** One who is without death or its cause.
199. **Sarvadṛk:** One who sees the Karma of all Jivas through His inherent wisdom.
200. **Simhaḥ:** One who does Himsa or destruction.
201. **Sandhātā:** One who unites the Jivas with the fruits of their actions.
202. **Sandhimān:** One who is the enjoyer of the fruits of actions.
203. **Sthiraḥ:** One who is always of the same nature.
204. **Ajaḥ:** The root 'Aj' means both 'go' and 'throw'. So the name means One who goes into the

hearts of devotees or One who throws the evil Asuras to a distance, i.e., destroys them.

205. **Durmarṣaṇaḥ:** One whose might the Asuras cannot bear.

206. **Śasta:** One who instructs and directs all through the scriptures.

207. **Vishrutatma:** One who is specially known through signifying terms like truth, knowledge, etc.

208. **Surārihā:** One who destroys the enemies of Suras or Devas.

गुरुर्गुरुतमो धाम
सत्यः सत्यपराक्रमः ।
निमिषोऽनिमिषः स्रग्वी
वाचस्पतिरुदारधीः ॥२३॥

gururgurutamō dhāmaḥ
satyaḥ satyaparākramaḥ,
nimiṣō nimiṣaḥ sragvī
vācaspatirudāradhīḥ. (23)

209. **Guruḥ:** The greatest teacher.
210. **Gurutamaḥ:** One who is the teacher of all forms of knowledge.
211. **Dhāma:** The Supreme Light.
212. **Satyaḥ:** One who is embodied as virtue of truth.
213. **Satyaparākamaḥ:** One of unfailing valour.
214. **Nimiṣaḥ:** One whose eyelids are closed in Yoga-nidra.
215. **Animiṣaḥ:** One who is ever awake.
216. **Sragvī:** One who has on Him the necklace called Vaijayanti, which is strung with the subtle aspects of the five elements.

217. **Vācaspatir-udāradhīḥ:** Being the master of Vak or word, i.e., knowledge, He is called so. As his intellect perceives everything, He is Udaradhih. Both these epithets together constitute one name.

अग्रणीर्ग्रामणीः श्रीमान्
न्यायो नेता समीरणः ।
सहस्रमूर्धा विश्वात्मा
सहस्राक्षः सहस्रपात् ।।२४।।

agraṇīrgrāmaṇīḥ śrīmān
nyāyō netā samīraṇaḥ,
sahasramūrdhā viśvātmā
sahasrākṣaḥ sahasrapāt. (24)

218. **Agraṇīḥ:** One who leads all liberation-seekers to the highest status.

219. **Grāmaṇīḥ:** One who has the command over Bhutagrama or the collectivity of all beings.

220. **Śrīmān:** One more resplendent than everything.

221. **Nyāyaḥ:** The consistency that runs through all ways of knowing and which leads one to the truth of non-duality.

222. **Netā:** One who moves this world of becoming.

223. **Sahasramūrdhā:** One with a thousand, i.e., innumerable, heads.

224. **Samīraṇaḥ:** One who in the form of breath keeps all living beings functioning.

225. **Viśvātmā:** The soul of the universe.

226. **Sahasrākṣaḥ:** One with a thousand or innumerable eyes.

227. **Sahasrapāt:** One with a thousand, i.e., innumerable, legs.

आवर्तनो निवृत्तात्मा
संवृतः सम्प्रमर्दनः ।
अहः संवर्तको
वह्निरनिलो धरणीधरः ।।२५।।

āvartanō nivṛttātmā saṁvṛtaḥ
saṁpramardanaḥ,
ahaḥ saṁvartakō
vahniranilō dharaṇīdharaḥ. (25)

228. **Āvrtanaḥ:** One who whirls round and round the Samsara-chakra, the wheel of Samsara or worldy existence.

229. **Nivṛttātmā:** One whose being is free or untouched by the bondage of Samsara.

230. **Saṁvṛtaḥ:** One who is covered by all-covering Avidya or ignorance.

231. **Sampramardanaḥ:** One who delivers destructive blows on all beings through His Vibhutis (power manifestation like Rudra, Yama, etc.).

232. **Ahaḥ-saṁvartakaḥ:** The Lord who, as the sun, regulates the succession of day and night.

233. **Vahniḥ:** One who as fire carries the offerings made to the Devas in sacrifices.

234. **Anilaḥ:** One who has no fixed residence.

235. **Dharaṇī-dharaḥ:** One who supports the worlds, Adisesha, elephants of the quarters, etc.

सुप्रसादः प्रसन्नात्मा
विश्वधृग्विश्वभुग्विभुः ।
सत्कर्ता सत्कृतः
साधुर्जह्नुर्नारायणो नरः ॥२६॥

suprasādaḥ prasannātmā
viśvadhṛgviśvabhugvibhuḥ,
satkartā satkṛtaḥ
sādhurjahnurnārāyaṇō naraḥ. (26)

236. **Suprasādaḥ:** One whose Prasada or mercy is uniquely wonderful because He gives salvation to Sisupala and others who try to harm Him.
237. **Prasannātmā:** One whose mind is never contaminated by Rajas or Tamas.
238. **Viśvadhṛg:** One who holds the universe by his power.
239. **Viśvabhug:** One who eats up or enjoys or protects the worlds.
240. **Vibhuḥ:** One who takes various forms.
241. **Satkartā:** One who offers benefits.

242. **Satkṛtaḥ:** One who is adored even by those who deserve adoration.

243. **Sādhuḥ:** One who acts according to justice.

244. **Jahnuḥ:** One who dissolves all beings in oneself at the time of dissolution.

245. **Nārāyaṇaḥ:** 'Nara' means Atman. Narayana means One having His residence in all beings.

246. **Naraḥ:** Human being.

असङ्ख्येयोऽप्रमेयात्मा
विशिष्टः शिष्टकृच्छुचिः ।
सिद्धार्थः सिद्धसङ्कल्पः
सिद्धिदः सिद्धिसाधनः ॥२७॥

asaṅkhyeyō'prameyātmā
viśiṣṭaḥ śiṣṭakṛcchuciḥ,
siddhārthaḥ siddhasaṅkalpaḥ
siddhidaḥ siddhisādhanaḥ. (27)

247. **Asaṅkhyeyaḥ:** One who has no Sankhya or differences of name and form.
248. **Aprameyātmā:** One whose nature cannot be grasped by any of the means of knowledge.
249. **Viśiṣṭaḥ:** One who excels at everything.
250. **Śiṣṭakṛt:** One who commands everything or One who protects Shishtas or good men.
251. **Suciḥ:** Pure
252. **Siddhārthaḥ:** One whose object is always fulfilled.
253. **Siddhasaṅkalpaḥ:** One whose resolutions are always fulfilled.

254. **Siddhidaḥ:** One who bestows Siddhi or fulfillment on all who practise disciplines, in accordance with their eligibility.

255. **Siddhisādhanaḥ:** One who brings fulfillment to works that deserve the same.

वृषाही वृषभो
विष्णुर्वृषपर्वा वृषोदरः ।
वर्धनो वर्धमानश्च
विविक्तः श्रुतिसागरः ॥२८॥

vṛṣāhī vṛṣabhō
viṣṇurvṛṣaparvā vṛṣōdaraḥ,
vardhanō vardhamānaśca
viviktaḥ śrutisāgaraḥ. (28)

256. **Vṛṣāhī:** 'Vrusha' means dharma or merit.

257. **Vṛṣābhaḥ:** One who showers on the devotees all that they pray for.

258. **Viṣṇuḥ:** One who pervades everything.

259. **Vṛṣaparva:** One who has given as steps (Parvas), observances of the nature of Dharma, to those who want to attain the supreme state.

260. **Vṛṣodaraḥ:** One whose abdomen showers offspring.

261. **Vardhanaḥ:** One who increases the ecstasy of His devotees

262. **Vardhamānaḥ:** One who multiplies in the form of the universe.

263. **Viviktaḥ:** One who is untouched and unaffected.

264. **Śrutisāgaraḥ:** One to whom all the shruti or Vedic words and sentences flow.

सुभुजो दुर्धरो वाग्मी
महेन्द्रो वसुदो वसुः ।
नैकरूपो बृहद्रूपः
शिपिविष्टः प्रकाशनः ।।२६।।

subhujō durdharō vāgmī
mahendrō vasudō vasuḥ,
naikarūpō bṛhadrūpaḥ
śipiviṣṭaḥ prakāśanaḥ. (29)

265. **Subhujaḥ:** One possessing excellent arms that protect the worlds.
266. **Durdharaḥ:** One who holds up the universe—a work which none else can do.
267. **Vāgmi:** One from whom the words constituting the Veda come out.
268. **Mahendraḥ:** The great Lord, i.e., the Supreme Being, who is the God of all gods.
269. **Vasudaḥ:** One who bestows riches.
270. **Vasuḥ:** One who is himself the Vasu.
271. **Naikarūpaḥ:** One who is without an exclusive form.

272. **Bṛhadrūpaḥ:** One who has adopted mysterious forms like that of a Boar.

273. **Śipiviṣṭaḥ:** 'Shipi' means cow. One who resides in cows as Yajna.

274. **Prakāśanaḥ:** One who illumines everthing.

ओजस्तेजोद्युतिधरः
प्रकाशात्मा प्रतापनः ।
ऋद्धः स्पष्टाक्षरो
मन्त्रश्चन्द्रांशुर्भास्करद्युतिः ॥३०॥

ōjastejōdyutidharaḥ
prakāśātmā pratāpanaḥ,
ṛddhaḥ spaṣṭākṣarō
mantraścandrāṁśurbhāskaradyutiḥ. (30)

275. **Ōjas-tejō-dyuti-dharaḥ:** One who is endowed with strength, vigour and brilliance.

276. **Prakāśātmā:** One whose form is radiant.

277. **Pratāpanaḥ:** One who warms the world through the power manifestations like the Sun.

278. **Ṛddhaḥ:** One who is rich in excellences like Dharma, Gyana (knowledge), Vairagya (renunciation), etc.

279. **Spaṣṭākṣaraḥ:** He is so called because Omkara, the manifesting sound of the Lord, is Spashta or high pitched.

280. **Mantraḥ:** One who manifests as the mantras.

281. **Candrāṁśuḥ:** He is called Chandramshu or moonlight because just as the moon-light gives relief to men burnt in the heat of the sun, He gives relief and shelter to those who are subjected to the heat of Samsara.

282. **Bhāskara-dyutiḥ:** He who has the effulgence of the sun.

अमृतांशूद्भवो भानुः
शशबिन्दुः सुरेश्वरः ।
औषधं जगतः सेतुः
सत्यधर्मपराक्रमः ॥३१॥

amṛtāṁśūdbhavō bhānuḥ
śaśabinduḥ sureśvaraḥ,
auṣadhaṁ jagataḥ setuḥ
satyadharmaparākramaḥ. (31)

283. **Amṛtāṁśūdbhavaḥ:** The Paramatman from whom Amrutamshu or the Moon originated at the time of the churning of the Milk Ocean.

284. **Bhānuḥ:** One who shines.

285. **Śaśabinduḥ:** The word means One who has the mark of the hare, i.e., the Moon.

286. **Sureśvaraḥ:** One who is the Lord of all Devas and those who do good.

287. **Auṣadham:** One who is the Aushadha or medicine for the great disease of Samsara.

288. **Jagataḥ setuḥ:** One who is the aid to go across the ocean of Samsara.

289. **Satya-dharma-parākramaḥ:** One whose excellences like righteousness, omniscience, puissance, etc. are all true.

भूतभव्यभवन्नाथः
पवनः पावनोऽनलः ।
कामहा कामकृत्कान्तः
कामः कामप्रदः प्रभुः ।।३२।।

bhūtabhavyabhavannāthaḥ
pavanaḥ pāvano’nalaḥ,
kāmahā kāmakṛtkāntaḥ
kāmaḥ kāmapradaḥ prabhuḥ. (32)

290. **Bhūta-bhavya-bhavan-nāthaḥ:** One who is the master for all the beings of the past, future and present.

291. **Pavanaḥ:** One who causes movement.

292. **Pāvanaḥ:** One who is the purifier.

293. **Analaḥ:** The Jivatma is called Anala because it recognizes Ana or Prana as Himself.

294. **Kāmahā:** One who destroys the desire-nature in seekers after liberation.

295. **Kāmakṛt:** One who fulfils the wants of pure minded devotees.

296. **Kantaḥ:** One who is extremely beautiful.

297. **Kāmaḥ:** One who is sought after by those who desire to attain the four supreme values of life.

298. **Kāmapradaḥ:** One who liberally fulfils the desires of devotees.

299. **Prabhuḥ:** One who surpasses all.

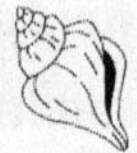

युगादिकृद्युगावर्तो
नैकमायो महाशनः ।
अदृश्यो व्यक्तरूपश्च
सहस्रजिदनन्तजित् ॥३३॥

yugādikṛdyugāvartō
naikamāyō mahāśanaḥ,
adṛśyō vyaktarūpaśca
sahasrajidanantajit. (33)

300. **Yugādikṛd:** One who is the cause of periods of time like Yuga.
301. **Yugāvartaḥ:** One who as time causes the repetition of the four Yugas beginning with Satya Yuga.
302. **Naikamāyaḥ:** One who can assume numerous forms of Maya, not one only.
303. **Mahāśanaḥ:** One who consumes everything at the end of a Kalpa.
304. **Adṛśyaḥ:** One who cannot be grasped by any of the five organs of knowledge.

305. **Vyaktarūpaḥ:** He is so called because His gross form as universe can be clearly perceived.

306. **Sahasrajit:** One who is victorious over innumerable enemies of the Devas in battle.

307. **Anantajit:** One who, being endowed with all powers, is victorious at all times over everything.

इष्टोऽविशिष्टः शिष्टेष्टः
शिखण्डी नहुषो वृषः ।
क्रोधहा क्रोधकृत्कर्ता
विश्वबाहुर्महीधरः ॥३४॥

iṣṭō'viśiṣṭaḥ śiṣṭeṣṭaḥ
śikhaṇḍī nahuṣō vṛṣaḥ,
krōdhahā krōdhakṛtkartā
viśvabāhurmahīdharaḥ. (34)

308. **Iṣṭaḥ:** One who is dear to all because He is of the nature of supreme bliss.
309. **Aviśiṣṭaḥ:** One who resides within all.
310. **Śiṣṭeṣṭaḥ:** One who is dear to Shishta or Knowing Ones.
311. **Śikhaṇḍī:** One who used a Sikhanda (feather of a peacock) for His crown's decoration when he adopted the form of a Gopa (cowherd).
312. **Nahuṣaḥ:** One who binds all beings by and through his Maya.
313. **Vṛṣaḥ:** One who is of the form of Dharma.

314. **Krōdhahā:** One who eradicates anger in virtuous people.

315. **Krōdhakṛt-kartā:** One who generates Krodha or anger in evil people.

316. **Viśvabāhuḥ:** One who is the support of all or One who has got all beings as His arms.

317. **Mahīdharaḥ:** 'Mahi' means both earth and worship. So the name means One who supports the earth or receives all forms of worship.

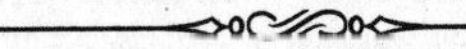

अच्युतः प्रथितः प्राणः
प्राणदो वासवानुजः ।
अपांनिधिरधिष्ठानमप्रमत्तः
प्रतिष्ठितः ॥३५॥

acyutaḥ prathitaḥ prāṇaḥ
prāṇadō vāsavānujaḥ,
apāṁnidhiradhiṣṭhānamapramattaḥ
pratiṣṭhitaḥ. (35)

318. **Acyutaḥ:** One who is without the six transformations beginning with birth.

319. **Prathitaḥ:** One who is famous because of His works like creation of the worlds etc.

320. **Prāṇaḥ:** One who, as Hiranyagarbha, endows all beings with Prana.

321. **Prāṇadaḥ:** One who bestows Prana, i.e., strength, on Devas and Asuras and also destroys them by withdrawing it.

322. **Vāsavānujaḥ:** One who was born as younger brother of Indra (Vasava) in His incarnation as Vamana.

323. **Apāṁ nidhiḥ:** The word means collectivity of water or the ocean.

324. **Adhiṣṭhānam:** The seat or support for everything.

325. **Apramattaḥ:** One who is always vigilant in awarding the fruits of actions to those who are entiled to them.

326. **Pratiṣṭhitaḥ:** One who is supported and established in His own greatness.

स्कन्दः स्कन्दधरो धुर्यो
वरदो वायुवाहनः ।
वासुदेवो बृहद्भानुरादिदेवः
पुरन्दरः ॥३६॥

skandaḥ skandadharō
dhuryō varadō vāyuvāhanaḥ,
vāsudevō bṛhadbhānurādidevaḥ
purandaraḥ. (36)

327. **Skandaḥ:** One who drives everything as air.
328. **Skanda-dharaḥ:** One who supports Skanda or the righteous path.
329. **Dhuryaḥ:** One who bears the burden of all beings.
330. **Varadaḥ:** One who gives boons.
331. **Vāyuvāhanaḥ:** One who vibrates the seven Vayus or atmospheres beginning with Avaha.
332. **Vāsudevaḥ:** One who is both Vasu and Deva.
333. **Bṛhadbhānuḥ:** The great brilliance.

334. **Ādidevaḥ:** The Divinity who is the source of all Devas.

335. **Purandaraḥ:** One who destroys the cities of the enemies of Devas.

अशोकस्तारणस्तारः शूरः
शौरिर्जनेश्वरः ।
अनुकूलः शतावर्तः
पद्मी पद्मनिभेक्षणः ॥३७॥

aśōkastāraṇastāraḥ śūraḥ
śaurirjaneśvaraḥ,
anukūlaḥ śatāvartaḥ
padmī padmanibhekṣaṇaḥ. (37)

336. **Aśokaḥ:** One without the six defects—sorrow, infatuation, hunger, thirst, birth and death.

337. **Tāraṇaḥ:** One who uplifts beings from the ocean of Samsara.

338. **Tāraḥ:** One who liberates beings from the fear of residence in the womb, birth, old age, death, etc.

339. **Śūraḥ:** One of great prowess, i.e., who fulfils the four supreme satisfactions of life—Dharma, Artha, Kama and Moksha.

340. **Śauriḥ:** One who as Krishna as the son of Sura, that is Vasudeva.

341. **Janeśvaraḥ:** The Lord of all beings.

342. **Anukūlaḥ:** One who, being the Atman of all beings, is favourable to all, for no one will act against oneself.

343. **Śatāvartaḥ:** One who has had several Avataras or incarnations.

344. **Padmī:** One having Padma or lotus in his hands.

345. **Padma-nibhekṣaṇaḥ:** One with eyes resembling lotus.

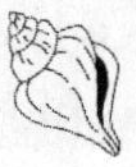

पद्मनाभोऽरविन्दाक्षः
पद्मगर्भः शरीरभृत् ।
महर्द्धिरृद्धो वृद्धात्मा
महाक्षो गरुडध्वजः ।।३८।।

padmanābhōravindākṣaḥ
padmagarbhaḥ śarīrabhṛt,
maharddhir ṛddhō vṛddhātmā
mahākṣō garuḍadhvajaḥ. (38)

346. **Padma-nābhaḥ:** One who resides in the Nabhi or the central part of the heart-lotus.
347. **Aravindākṣaḥ:** One whose eyes resemble Aravinda or the Lotus.
348. **Padma-garbhaḥ:** One who is fit to be worshipped in the middle of the heart-lotus.
349. **Śarīra-bhṛt:** One who supports the bodies of beings, strengthening them in the form of Anna (food) and Prana.
350. **Mahardhi:** One who has enormous Ruddhi or prosperity.
351. **Ṛddhaḥ:** One who is seen as standing in the form of the world.

352. **Vṛddhātmā:** One whose Atma or body is Vruddha or ancient.

353. **Mahākṣaḥ:** One who has got two or many glorious eyes.

354. **Garuḍa-dhvajaḥ:** One who has got Garuda as his flag.

अतुलः शरभो भीमः
समयज्ञो हविर्हरिः ।
सर्वलक्षणलक्षण्यो
लक्ष्मीवान् समितिञ्जयः ।।३६।।

atulaḥ śarabhō bhīmaḥ
samayajñō havirhariḥ,
sarvalakṣaṇalakṣaṇyō
lakṣmīvān samitiñjayaḥ. (39)

355. **Atulaḥ:** One who cannot be compared to anything else.
356. **Śarabhaḥ:** He who shines within all bodies that is Sarabhah.
357. **Bhīmaḥ:** One of whom everyone is afraid.
358. **Samayajñaḥ:** One who knows the time for creation, sustenance and dissolution.
359. **Havir-hariḥ:** One who takes the portion of offerings (Havis) in Yajnas.
360. **Sarva-lakṣaṇa-lakṣaṇyaḥ:** The supreme knowledge obtained through all criteria of knowledge, i.e., Paramatma.

361. **Lakṣmīvān:** One on whose chest Goddess Lakshmi is always residing.

362. **Samitiñjayaḥ:** One who is vicotious in Samiti or war.

विक्षरो रोहितो मार्गो
हेतुर्दामोदरः सहः ।
महीधरो महाभागो
वेगवानमिताशनः ॥४०॥

\vikṣarō rōhitō mārgō
heturdamodarassahaḥ,
mahīdharō mahābhāgō
vegavānamitāśanaḥ. (40)

363. **Vikṣaraḥ:** One who is without Kshara or desruction.

364. **Rōhitaḥ:** One who assumed the form of a kind of fish called Rohita.

365. **Mārgaḥ:** One who is sought after by persons seeking Moksha.

366. **Hetuḥ:** One who is both the instrumental and the material cause of the universe.

367. **Damodaraḥ:** One who has very benevolent mind because of disciplines like self-control.

368. **Sahaḥ:** One who subordinates everything.

369. **Mahīdharaḥ:** One who props up the earth in the form of mountain.

370. **Mahābhāgaḥ:** He who, taking a body by His own will, enjoys supreme felicities.

371. **Vegavān:** One of tremendous speed.

372. **Amitāśanaḥ:** He who consumes all the worlds at the time of Dissolution.

उद्भवः क्षोभणो देवः
श्रीगर्भः परमेश्वरः ।
करणं कारणं कर्ता
विकर्ता गहनो गुहः ।।४१।।

udbhavaḥ, kṣōbhaṇō devaḥ
śrīgarbhaḥ parameśvaraḥ,
karaṇaṁ kāraṇaṁ kartā
vikartā gahanō guhaḥ. (41)

373. **Udbhavaḥ:** One who is the material cause of creation.

374. **Kṣōbhaṇaḥ:** One who at the time of creation entered into the Purusha and Prakriti and caused agitation.

375. **Devaḥ:** Divine being.

376. **Śrīgarbhaḥ:** One in whose Garbha (abdomen) Shri or His unique manifestation as Samsara has its existence.

377. **Parameśvaraḥ:** 'Parama' means the supreme. 'Ishvarah' means One who hold sway over all beings.

378. **Karaṇam:** He who is the most important factor in the generation of this universe.

379. **Kāraṇam:** The Cause—He who causes others to act.

380. **Kartā:** One who is free and is, therefore, one's own master.

381. **Vikartā:** One who makes this unique universe.

382. **Gahanaḥ:** One whose nature, greatness and actions cannot be known by anybody.

383. **Guhaḥ:** One who hides His own nature with the help of His power of Maya.

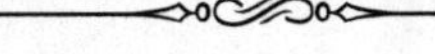

व्यवसायो व्यवस्थानः
संस्थानः स्थानदो ध्रुवः ।
परर्द्धिः परमस्पष्टस्तुष्टः
पुष्टः शुभेक्षणः ॥४२॥

vyavasāyō vyavasthānaḥ
saṁsthānaḥ sthānadō dhruvaḥ,
pararddhiḥ paramaspaṣṭastuṣṭaḥ
puṣṭaḥ śubhekṣaṇaḥ. (42)

384. **Vyavasāyaḥ:** One who is wholly of the nature of knowledge.
385. **Vyavasthānaḥ:** He in whom the orderly regulation of the universe rests.
386. **Sāṁsthānaḥ:** One in whom all beings dwell in the states of dissolution.
387. **Sthānadaḥ:** One who gives their particular status to persons like Dhruva according to their Karma.
388. **Dhruvaḥ:** One who is indestructible.
389. **Pararddhiḥ:** One who possesses lordliness of this most exalted type.

390. **Paramaspaṣṭaḥ:** One in whom 'Para' or supremely glorious 'Ma' or Lakshmi dwells or One who is the greatest of all beings without any other's help.

391. **Tuṣṭaḥ:** One who is of the nature of supreme.

392. **Puṣṭaḥ:** One who in fills everything.

393. **Śubhekṣaṇaḥ:** One whose Ikshanam or vision bestows good on all beings i.e., gives liberation to those who want Moksha and enjoyments to those who are after it, and also cuts asunder the knots of the heart by eliminating all doubts.

रामो विरामो विरजो मार्गो
नेयो नयोऽनयः ।
वीरः शक्तिमतां श्रेष्ठो
धर्मो धर्मविदुत्तमः ।।४३।।

rāmō virāmō virajō mārgō
neyō nayōnayaḥ,
vīraḥ śaktimatāṁ śreṣṭhō
dharmō dharmaviduttamaḥ. (43)

394. **Ramaḥ:** The eternally blissful on in whom the Yogis find delight.
395. **Virāmaḥ:** One in whom the Virama or end of all beings takes place.
396. **Virajaḥ:** One in whom the desire for enjoyments has ceased
397. **Mārgaḥ:** The path.
398. **Neyaḥ:** One who directs or leads the Jiva to the Supreme Being through spiritual realization.
399. **Nayaḥ:** One who leads, i.e., who is the leader in the form of spiritual illumination.
400. **Anayaḥ:** One for whom there is no leader.

401. **Vīraḥ:** One who is valorous.

402. **Śaktimatāṁ śreṣṭhaḥ:** One who is the most powerful among all powerful beings like Brahma.

403. **Dharmaḥ:** One who supports all beings.

404. **Dharma-viduttamaḥ:** The greatest of knower of Dharma. He is called so because all the scriptures consisting of Shrutis and Smrutis form His commandments.

वैकुण्ठः पुरुषः प्राणः
प्राणदः प्रणवः पृथुः ।
हिरण्यगर्भः शत्रुघ्नो
व्याप्तो वायुरधोक्षजः ॥४४॥

vaikuṇṭhaḥ puruṣaḥ prāṇaḥ
prāṇadaḥ praṇavaḥ pṛthuḥ,
hiraṇyagarbhaḥ śatrughnō
vyāptō vāyuradhōkṣajaḥ. (44)

405. **Vaikuṇṭhaḥ:** The bringing together of the diversified categories is Vikuntha. He who is the agent of it is Vaikunthah.

406. **Puruṣaḥ:** One who existed before everything.

407. **Prāṇaḥ:** One who lives as Kshetrajana (knower in the body) or One who functions in the form of vital force called Prana.

408. **Prāṇadaḥ:** One who is the giver of life.

409. **Praṇavaḥ:** One who is praised or to whom prostration is made with Om.

410. **Pṛthuḥ:** One who has expanded himself as the world.

411. **Hiraṇyagarbhaḥ:** He who was the cause of the golden-coloured egg out of which Brahma was born.

412. **Śatrughnaḥ:** One who destroys the enemies of the Devas.

413. **Vyāptaḥ:** One who as the cause pervades all effects.

414. **Vāyuḥ:** One who moves towards His devotees.

415. **Adhokṣajaḥ:** He is Adhokshaja because he undergoes no degeneration from His original nature.

ऋतुः सुदर्शनः कालः
परमेष्ठी परिग्रहः ।
उग्रः संवत्सरो दक्षो
विश्रामो विश्वदक्षिणः ।।४५।।

ṛtuḥ sudarśanaḥ kālaḥ
parameṣṭhī parigrahaḥ,
ugraḥ saṁvatsarō dakṣō
viśrāmō viśvadakṣiṇaḥ. (45)

416. **Ṛtuḥ:** One who is of the nature of Kala (time) that is indicated by the word Ritu or season.

417. **Sudarśanaḥ:** One whose Darshana or vision that is knowledge, bestows the most auspicious fruit Moksha.

418. **Kālaḥ:** One who measures and sets a limit to everything.

419. **Parameṣṭhī:** One who dwells in his supreme greatness in the sky of the heart.

420. **Parigrahaḥ:** One who, being everywhere, is grasped on all sides by those who seek refuge in Him or One who grasps or receives the offerings made by devotees.

421. **Ugraḥ:** One who is the cause of fear to even beings like Sun.

422. **Saṁvatsaraḥ:** One in whom all beings reside.

423. **Dakṣaḥ:** One who augments in the form of the world.

424. **Viśrāmaḥ:** One who bestows Vishrama or liberation to aspirants who seek relief from the ocean of Samsara with its waves of various tribulations in the from of hunger, thirst, etc., and difficulties like Avidya, pride, infatuation, etc.

425. **Viśvadakṣiṇaḥ:** One who is more skilled (Daksha) than everyone or One who is proficient in everything.

विस्तारः स्थावरस्थाणुः
प्रमाणं बीजमव्ययम् ।
अर्थोऽनर्थो महाकोशो
महाभोगो महाधनः ।।४६।।

vistāraḥ sthāvaraḥsthāṇuḥ
pramāṇaṁ bījamavyayam,
arthōnarthō mahākōśō
mahābhōgō mahādhanaḥ. (46)

426. **Vistāraḥ:** One in whom all the worlds have attained manifestation.

427. **Sthāvaraḥ-sthāṇuḥ:** One who is firmly established is Sthavara, and in whom long lasting entities like earth are established in Sthanu. The Lord is both these.

428. **Pramāṇaṁ:** One who is of the nature of pure consciousness.

429. **Bījamavyayam:** One who is the seed or cause of Samsara without Himself undergoing any change.

430. **Arthaḥ:** One who is sought (Arthita) by all, as He is of the nature of bliss.

431. **Anarthaḥ:** One who, being self-fulfilled, has no other Artha or end to seek.

432. **Mahākōśaḥ:** One who has got as His covering the great Koshas like Annamaya, Pranamaya, etc.

433. **Mahābhōgaḥ:** One who has Bliss as the great source of enjoyment.

434. **Mahādhanaḥ:** One who has got the whole universe as the wealth (Dhana) for His enjoyment.

अनिर्विण्णः स्थविष्ठोऽभूर्धर्मयूपो
महामखः ।
नक्षत्रनेमिर्नक्षत्री
क्षमः क्षामः समीहनः ।।४७।।

anirviṇṇaḥ sthaviṣṭhōbhūrdharmayūpō
mahāmakhaḥ.
nakṣatranemirnakṣatrī
kṣamaḥ kṣāmaḥ samīhanaḥ. (47)

435. **Anirviṇṇaḥ:** One who is never heedless, because He is ever self-fulfilled.

436. **Sthaviṣṭhaḥ:** One of huge proportions because He is in the form of cosmic person.

437. **Abhūḥ:** One without birth or One has no existence.

438. **Dharma-yūpaḥ:** The sacrificial post for Dharmas, i.e., One to whom all the forms of Dharma, which are His own form of worship, are attached, just as a sacrificial animal is attached to a Yupa or a sacrificial post.

439. **Mahāmakhaḥ:** One by offering sacrifices to whom, those sacrifices deserve to be called great, because they well give the fruit of Nirvana.

440. **Nakṣatra-nemiḥ:** The heart of all nakshatras.

441. **Nakṣatrī:** He is in the form of the nakshatra.

442. **Kṣamaḥ:** One who is clever in everything.

443. **Kṣāmaḥ:** One who remains in the state of pure self after all the modifications of the mind have dwindled.

444. **Samīhanaḥ:** One who exerts well for creation, etc.

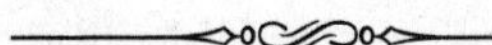

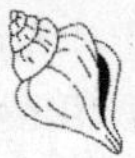

यज्ञ इज्यो महेज्यश्च क्रतुः
सत्रं सतां गतिः ।
सर्वदर्शी विमुक्तात्मा
सर्वज्ञो ज्ञानमुत्तमम् ॥४८॥

yajña ijyō mahejyaśca kratuḥ
satraṁ satāṁ gatiḥ,
sarvadarśī vimuktātmā
sarvajñō jñānamuttamam. (48)

445. **Yajñaḥ:** One who is all-knowing.
446. **Ijayaḥ:** One who is fit to be worshipped in sacrifices.
447. **Mahejyaḥ:** He who, of all deities worshipped, is alone capable of giving the blessing of liberation.
448. **Kratuḥ:** A Yajna in which there is a sacrificial post is Kratu.
449. **Satraṁ:** One who is of the nature of ordained Dharma.
450. **Satāṁ-gatiḥ:** One who is the sole support for holy men who are seekers of Moksha.

451. **Sarva-darśī:** One who by His inborn insight is able to see all good and evil actions of living beings.

452. **Vimuktātmā:** One who is naturally free.

453. **Sarvagñaḥ:** One who is all and also the knower of all.

454. **Jñānam-uttamam:** That consciousness which is superior to all, birthless, unlimited by time and space and the cause of all achievements.

सुव्रतः सुमुखः सूक्ष्मः
सुघोषः सुखदः सुहृत् ।
मनोहरो जितक्रोधो
वीरबाहुर्विदारणः ॥४९॥

suvrataḥ sumukhaḥ sūkṣmaḥ
sughōṣaḥ sukhadaḥ suhṛt,
manōharō jitakrōdhō
vīrabāhurvidāraṇaḥ. (49)

455. **Suvrataḥ:** One who has take the magnanimous vow to save all refuge-seekers.
456. **Sumukhaḥ:** One with a pleasant face.
457. **Sūkṣmaḥ:** One who is subtle because He is without any gross causes like sound, etc.
458. **Sughōṣaḥ:** One whose auspicious sound is the Veda or One who has got a deep and sonorous sound like the clouds.
459. **Sukhadaḥ:** One who gives happiness to good people.
460. **Suhṛt:** One who helps without looking for any return.
461. **Manōharaḥ:** One who attracts the mind by

His incomparable blissful nature.

462. **Jitakrōdhaḥ:** One who has overcome anger.

463. **Vīrabāhuḥ:** One whose arms are capable of heroic deeds as demonstrated in his destruction of Asuras for establishing Vedic Dharma.

464. **Vidāraṇaḥ:** One who destroys those who live contrary to Dharma.

स्वापनः स्ववशो व्यापी
नैकात्मा नैककर्मकृत् ।
वत्सरो वत्सलो वत्सी
रत्नगर्भो धनेश्वरः ॥५०॥

svāpanaḥ svavaśo vyāpī
naikātmā naikakarmakṛt,
vatsaro vatsalo vatsī
ratnagarbho dhaneśvaraḥ. (50)

465. **Svāpanaḥ:** One who enfolds the Jivas in the sleep of Ajnana.

466. **Svavaśaḥ:** One who is dominated by oneself and not anything else as He is the cause of the whole cosmic process.

467. **Vyāpī:** One who interpenetrates everything like Akasha.

468. **Naikātmā:** One who manifests in different forms as the subsidiary agencies causing the various cosmic processes.

469. **Naikakarmakṛt:** One who engages in innumerable activities in the process of creation, sustenance, etc.

470. **Vatsaraḥ:** One in whom everything dwells.

471. **Vatsalaḥ:** One who has love for His devotees.

472. **Vatsī:** One who protects those who are dear to Him.

473. **Ratnagarbhaḥ:** The Ocean is called so because gems are found in its depths. As the Lord has taken the form of the ocean, He is called by this name.

474. **Dhaneśvaraḥ:** One who is the Lord of all wealth.

धर्मगुब्धर्मकृद्धर्मी
सदसत्क्षरमक्षरम् ।
अविज्ञाता सहस्रांशुर्विधाता
कृतलक्षणः ॥५१॥

dharmagubdharmakṛddharmī
sadasatkṣaramakṣaram,
avijñātā sahasrāṁśurvidhātā
kṛtalakṣaṇaḥ. (51)

475. **Dharmagub:** One who protects Dharma.

476. **Dharmakṛd:** Though above Dharma and Adharma, He performs Dharma in order to keep up the traditions in respect of it.

477. **Dharmī:** One who upholds Dharma.

478. **Sat:** The Parabrahman who is of the nature of truth.

479. **Asat:** As the Aparabrahma has manifested as the world He is called Asat (not having reality).

480. **Kṣaram:** All beings subjected to change.

481. **Akṣaram:** The changeless one.

482. **Aviñātā:** One who is without the attributes of a Jiva or vigyata like sense of agency, etc.

483. **Sahasrāṁśuḥ:** One with numerous rays, i.e., the sun.

484. **Vidhātā:** One who is the unique support of all agencies like Ananta who bear the whole universe.

485. **Kṛtalakṣaṇaḥ:** One who is of the nature of conscousness.

गभस्तिनेमिः सत्त्वस्थः
सिंहो भूतमहेश्वरः ।
आदिदेवो महादेवो
देवेशो देवभृद्गुरुः ।।५२।।

gabhastinemiḥ sattvasthaḥ
siṁhō bhūtamaheśvaraḥ,
ādidevō mahādevō
deveśō devabhṛdguruḥ. (52)

486. **Gabhastinemiḥ:** He who dwells in the middle of Gabhasti or rays as the Sun.

487. **Sattvasthaḥ:** One who dwells especially in sattvaguna, which is luminous by nature.

488. **Simhaḥ:** One who has irresistible power like a lion.

489. **Bhūtamaheśvaraḥ:** The Supreme Lord of all beings.

490. **Ādidevaḥ:** He who is the first of all beings.

491. **Mahādevaḥ:** One whose greatness consists in His supreme self-knowledge.

492. **Deveśaḥ:** One who is the lord of all Devas, being the most important among them.

493. **Devabhṛd-guruḥ:** Indra who governs the Devas is Devabhrut. The Lord is even that Indra's controller (Guru).

उत्तरो गोपतिर्गोप्ता
ज्ञानगम्यः पुरातनः ।
शरीरभूतभृद्भोक्ता
कपीन्द्रो भूरिदक्षिणः ।।५३।।

uttarō gōpatirgōptā
jñānagamyaḥ purātanaḥ,
śarīrabhūtabhṛdbhōktā
kapīndrō bhūridakṣiṇaḥ. (53)

494. **Uttaraḥ:** One who is Uttirna or liberated from Samsara.

495. **Gōpatiḥ:** Krishna, who tends the cattle in the form of a Gopa. One who is the master of the earth.

496. **Gōptā:** One who is the protector of all beings.

497. **Jñānagamyaḥ:** The Lord cannot be known through Karma or a combination of Karma and Jyana.

498. **Purātanaḥ:** One who is not limited by time and who existed before anything else.

499. **Śarīrabhūtabhṛd:** One who is the master of the five Bhutas (elements) of which the body is made.

500. **Bhōktā:** One who protects or One who is the enjoyer of infinite bliss.

501. **Kapīndraḥ:** Kapi is a reference to the great Varaha, and 'Indra' means master or leader or superior. Therefore, Kapindrah is a reference to the great Varaha Avatara of Vishnu. Kapi is also a reference to monkey or Vanara. Therefore, 'Kapindrah' means One who is the leader of the monkeys or Vanaras and, therefore, a reference to Shri Raghava or Shri Rama.

502. **Bhūridakṣiṇaḥ:** One to whom numerous Dakshinas or votive offerings are made in Yajnas.

सोमपोऽमृतपः सोमः
पुरुजित्पुरुसत्तमः ।
विनयो जयः सत्यसन्धो
दाशार्हः सात्वताम्पतिः ॥५४॥

somapo'mṛtapaḥ sōmaḥ
purujit purusattamaḥ,
vinayō jayaḥ satyasandhō
dāśārha ssātvatāṁ patiḥ. (54)

503. **Sōmapaḥ:** One who drinks the Soma in all Yajnas in the form of the Devata.

504. **Amṛtapaḥ:** One who drinks the drink of immortal Bliss which is of one's own nature.

505. **Sōmaḥ:** One who as the moon invigorates the plants.

506. **Purujit:** One who gains victory over numerous people.

507. **Purushottamaḥ:** As His form is of cosmic dimension, He is Puru or great, and as He is the most important of all, He is Sattama.

508. **Vinayaḥ:** One who inflicts Vinaya or punishment on evil ones.

509. **Jayaḥ:** One who is victorious over all beings.

510. **Satyasandhaḥ:** One whose Sandha or resolve becomes always true.

511. **Dāśārhaḥ:** 'Dasha' means charitable offering. Therefore, He to whom charitable offerings deserve to be made.

512. **Sātvatāṁ-patiḥ:** Sattvatam is the name of a Tantra. So, the One who gave it out or commented upon it.

जीवो विनयिता साक्षी
मुकुन्दोऽमितविक्रमः ।
अम्भोनिधिरनन्तात्मा
महोदधिशयोऽन्तकः ॥५५॥

jīvo vinayitā sākṣī
mukundo'mitavikramaḥ,
ambhonidhiranantātmā
mahodadhiśayo'ntakaḥ. (55)

513. **Jīvaḥ:** One who as the Kshetragya or knower of the field or the body, is associated with the Pranas.

514. **Vinayitā-sākṣī:** One who witnesses the Vinayita or worshipful attitude of all devotees.

515. **Mukundaḥ:** One who bestows Mukti or liberation.

516. **Amitavikramaḥ:** One whose three strides were limitless.

517. **Ambhōnidhiḥ:** One in whom the Ambas or all beings from Devas down dwell.

518. **Anantātmā:** One who cannot be determined by space, time and causation.

519. **Mahōdadhi-śayaḥ:** One who lies in the water of cosmic dissolution into which all entities in the universe have been dissolved.

520. **Antakaḥ:** One who brings about the end of all beings.

अजो महार्हः स्वाभाव्यो
जितामित्रः प्रमोदनः ।
आनन्दो नन्दनो नन्दः
सत्यधर्मा त्रिविक्रमः ।।५६।।

ajō mahārhaḥ svābhāvyō
jitāmitraḥ pramōdanaḥ,
ānandō nandanō nandaḥ
satyadharmā trivikramaḥ. (56)

521. **Ajaḥ:** 'A' means Mahavishnu. So the word means One who is born of Vishnu, i.e., Kama Deva.

522. **Mahārhaḥ:** One who is fit for worship.

523. **Svābhāvyaḥ:** Being eternally perfect He is naturally without a beginning.

524. **Jitāmitraḥ:** One who has conquered the inner enemies like attachment, anger, etc., as also external enemies like Ravana, Kumbhakarna, etc.

525. **Pramōdanaḥ:** One who is always joyous as He is absorbed in immortal Bliss.

526. **Ānandaḥ:** One whose form is Ananda or Bliss.

527. **Nandanaḥ:** One who gives delight.

528. **Nandaḥ:** One endowed with all perfections.

529. **Satyadharmā:** One whose knowledge and other attributes are true.

530. **Trivikramaḥ:** One whose three strides covered the whole world.

महर्षिः कपिलाचार्यः
कृतज्ञो मेदिनीपतिः ।
त्रिपदस्त्रिदशाध्यक्षो
महाशृङ्गः कृतान्तकृत् ॥५७॥

maharṣiḥ kapilācāryaḥ
kṛtajñō medinīpatiḥ,
tripadastridaśādhyakṣō
mahāśṛṅgaḥ kṛtāntakṛt. (57)

531. **Maharṣiḥ Kapilācāryaḥ:** Kapila is called Maharshi because he was master of all the Vedas.

532. **Kṛtajñaḥ:** 'Kruta' means the world because it is of the nature of an effect.

533. **Medinīpatiḥ:** One who is the Lord of the earth.

534. **Tripadaḥ:** One having three strides.

535. **Tridaśādhyakṣaḥ:** One who is the witness of the three states of waking, dreaming and sleeping, which spring from the influence of the Gunas.

536. **Mahāśṛṅgaḥ:** One with a great antenna.

537. **Kṛtānta-kṛt:** One who brings about the destruction of the Kruta or the manifested condition of the universse.

महावराहो गोविन्दः
सुषेणः कनकाङ्गदी ।
गुह्यो गभीरो गहनो
गुप्तश्चक्रगदाधरः ॥५८॥

mahāvarāhō gōvindaḥ
suṣeṇaḥ kanakāṅgadī,
guhyō gabhīrō gahanō
guptaścakragadādharaḥ. (58)

538. **Mahā-varāhaḥ:** The great Cosmic Boar.

539. **Gōvindaḥ:** 'Go' means words, i.e., the Vedic sentences. He who is known by them is Gōvindaḥ.

540. **Suṣeṇaḥ:** One who has got about Him an armed guard in the shape of His eternal associates.

541. **Kanakāṅgadī:** One who has Angadas (armlets) made of gold.

542. **Guhyaḥ:** One who is to be known by the Guhya or the esoteric knowledge conveyed by the Upanishads or One who is hidden in the Guha or heart.

543. **Gabhīraḥ:** One who is of profound majesty because of attributes like omniscience, lordliness, strength, prowess, etc.

544. **Gahanaḥ:** One who could be entered into only with great difficulty. One who is the witness of the three states of waking, dreaming and sleeping, as also their absence.

545. **Guptaḥ:** One who is not an object of words, thought, etc.

546. **Chakra-gadā-dharaḥ:** One who has discus and Gada in hand.

वेधाः स्वाङ्गोऽजितः कृष्णो
दृढः सङ्कर्षणोऽच्युतः ।
वरुणो वारुणो वृक्षः
पुष्कराक्षो महामनाः ॥५९॥

vedhāḥ svāṅgo'jitaḥ kṛṣṇo
dṛḍhaḥ saṅkarṣaṇo'cyutaḥ,
varuṇo vāruṇo vṛukṣaḥ
puṣkarākṣo mahāmanāḥ. (59)

547. **Vedhāḥ:** One who does Vidhana or regulation.
548. **Svāṅgaḥ:** One who is oneself the participant in accomplishing works.
549. **Ajitaḥ:** One who has not been conquered by anyone in His various incarnations.
550. **Kṛṣṇaḥ:** One who is known as Krishna-dvaipayana.
551. **Dṛḍhaḥ:** One whose nature and capacity know no decay.
552. **Saṅkarṣaṇo-acyutaḥ:** Sankarshana is One who attracts to Oneself all beings at the time of cosmic dissolution, and Acyuta is One who

knows no fall from His real nature. They form one word with the first as the qualification—Acyuta who is Sankarshana.

553. **Varuṇaḥ:** The evening sun is called Varuna because he withdraws his rays into himself.

554. **Vāruṇaḥ:** Vasishta or Agastya, the sons of Varuna.

555. **Vṛukṣaḥ:** One who is unshakable like a tree.

556. **Puṣkarākṣaḥ:** One who shines as the light of consciousness when meditated upon in the lotus of the heart or One who has eyes resembling the lotus.

557. **Mahāmanāḥ:** One who fulfils the three functions of creation, sustenance and dissolution of the universe by the mind alone.

भगवान् भगहाऽऽनन्दी
वनमाली हलायुधः ।
आदित्यो ज्योतिरादित्यः
सहिष्णुर्गतिसत्तमः ॥६०॥

bhagavān bhagahānandī
vanamālī halāyudhaḥ,
ādityō jyōtirādityaḥ
sahiṣṇurgatisattamaḥ. (60)

558. **Bhagavān:** The origin, dissolution, the bondage and salvation of creatures, knowledge, ignorance—One who knows all these is Bhagavan.
559. **Bhagahā:** One who withdraws the Bhagas, beginning with lordliness, into Himself at the time of dissolution.
560. **Ānandī:** One whose nature is Ananda.
561. **Vanamālī:** One who wears the floral wreath (Vanamala) called Vaijayanti, which consists of the categories of five elements.
562. **Halāyudhaḥ:** One who in His incarnation as

Balabhadra had Hala or ploughshare as His weapon.

563. **Ādityaḥ:** One who was born of Aditi in His incarnation as Vamana.

564. **Jyōtir-ādityaḥ:** One who dwells in the brilliance of the sun's orb.

565. **Sahiṣṇuḥ:** One who puts up with the contraries like heat and cold.

566. **Gatisattamaḥ:** One who is the ultimate resort and support of all, and the greatest of all beings.

सुधन्वा खण्डपरशुर्दारुणो
द्रविणप्रदः ।
दिवस्पृक् सर्वदृग्व्यासो
वाचस्पतिरयोनिजः ॥६१॥

sudhanvā khaṇḍaparaśurdāruṇō
draviṇapradaḥ,
divaspṛk sarvadṛgvyāsō
vācaspatirayōnijaḥ. (61)

567. **Sudhanvā:** One who has got as His weapon the bow named Saranga of great excellence.

568. **Khaṇda-paraśuḥ:** The battle-axe that destroys enemies.

569. **Dāruṇaḥ:** One who is harsh and merciless to those who are on the evil path.

570. **Draviṇapradaḥ:** One who bestows the desired wealth on devotees.

571. **Divah-spṛk:** One who touches the heavens.

572. **Sarvadṛg-vyāsaḥ:** One whose comprehension includes everything in its ambit.

573. **Vācaspatirayōnijaḥ:** The Lord is Vachaspati because He is the master of all learning. He is Ayonija because He was not born of a mother. This forms a noun in combination with the attribute.

त्रिसामा सामगः साम
निर्वाणं भेषजं भिषक् ।
संन्यासकृच्छमः शान्तो
निष्ठा शान्तिः परायणम् ।।६२।।

trisāmā sāmagaḥ sāma
nirvāṇaṁ bheṣajaṁ bhiṣak,
saṁnyāsakṛcchamaśyāntō
niṣṭhā śāntiḥ parāyaṇam. (62)

574. **Trisāmā:** One who is praised by the chanters of Sama-gana through the three Samas known as Devavratam.

575. **Sāmagaḥ:** One who chants the Sama-gana.

576. **Sāma:** One who is Sama Veda.

577. **Nirvāṇaṁ:** That in which all miseries cease and which is of the nature of supreme bliss.

578. **Bheṣajaṁ:** The medicine for the disease of Samsara.

579. **Bhiṣak:** The Lord is called Bhishak or physician.

580. **Saṁnyāsakṛt:** One who instituted the fourth Ashrama of Sanyasa for the attainment of Moksha.

581. **Samaḥ:** One who has ordained the pacification of the mind as the most important discipline for Sannyasins (ascetics).

582. **Sāntaḥ:** The peaceful, being without interest in pleasures of the world.

583. **Niṣṭhā:** One in whom all beings remain in abeyance at the time of Pralaya.

584. **Śāntiḥ:** One in whom there is complete erasure of Avidya (ignorance).

585. **Parāyaṇam:** The state, which is the highest and from which there is no return to lower states.

शुभाङ्गः शान्तिदः स्रष्टा
कुमुदः कुवलेशयः ।
गोहितो गोपतिर्गोप्ता
वृषभाक्षो वृषप्रियः ॥६३॥

śubhāṅgaḥ śāntidaḥ sraṣṭā
kumudaḥ kuvaleśayaḥ,
gōhitō gōpatirgōptā
vṛṣabhākṣō vṛṣapriyaḥ. (63)

586. **Śubhāṅgaḥ:** One with a handsome form.

587. **Śāntidaḥ:** One who bestows Shanti, i.e., a state of freedom from attachment, antagonism, etc.

588. **Sraṣṭā:** One who brought forth everything at the start of the creative cycle.

589. **Kumudaḥ:** 'Ku' means the earth. So, One who revels in the pleasures of the earth.

590. **Kuvaleśayaḥ:** 'Kuvala' means water. One who lies in water is Kuvalesaya. 'Kuvala' also means the underside of serpents. One who lies on a serpent known as Adisesha is Kuvalesaya.

591. **Gōhitaḥ:** One who protected the cows by uplifting the mount Govardhana in His incarnation as Krishna.

592. **Gōpatiḥ:** The Lord of the earth.

593. **Gōptā:** One who is the protector of the earth or One who hides Himself by His Maya.

594. **Vṛṣapriyaḥ:** One whose eyes can rain all desirable objects on devotees. 'Vrushabha' means Dharma. So, One whose look is Dharma.

595. **Vrushapriyaḥ:** One to whom Vrusha or Dharma is dear.

अनिवर्ती निवृत्तात्मा
सङ्क्षेप्ता क्षेमकृच्छिवः ।
श्रीवत्सवक्षाः श्रीवासः
श्रीपतिः श्रीमतांवरः ॥६४॥

anivartī nivṛttātmā
saṁkṣeptā kṣemakṛcchivaḥ,
śrīvatsavakṣāḥ śrīvāsaḥ
śrīpatiḥ śrīmatāṁ varaḥ. (64)

596. **Anivartī:** One who never retreats in the battle with Asuras or One who, being devoted to Dharma, never abandons it.

597. **Nivṛttātmā:** One whose mind is naturally withdrawn from the objects of senses.

598. **Saṁkṣeptā:** One who at the time of cosmic dissolution contracts the expansive universe into a subtle state.

599. **Kṣemakṛt:** One who gives Kshema or protection to those that go to him.

600. **Śivaḥ:** One who purifies everyone by the very utterance of His name.

601. **Śrīvatsavakṣāḥ:** One on whose chest there is a mark called Shrivasta.

602. **Śrīvāsaḥ:** One on whose chest Shridevi always dwells.

603. **Śrīpatiḥ:** One whom at the time of the churning of the Milk Ocean Shridevi chose as her consort, rejecting all other Devas and Asuras. One who is the master of Shri (supreme cosmic power).

604. **Śrīmatāṁ-varaḥ:** One who is supreme over all deities like Brahma who are endowed with power and wealth of the Vedas.

श्रीदः श्रीशः श्रीनिवासः
श्रीनिधिः श्रीविभावनः ।
श्रीधरः श्रीकरः श्रेयः
श्रीमाँल्लोकत्रयाश्रयः ॥६५॥

śrīdaḥ śrīśaḥ śrīnivāsaḥ
śrīnidhiḥ śrīvibhāvanaḥ,
śrīdharaḥ śrīkaraḥ śreyaḥ
śrīmānlōkatrayāśrayaḥ. (65)

605. **Śrīdaḥ:** One who bestows prosperity on devotees.

606. **Śrīśaḥ:** One who is Lord of Goddess Shri.

607. **Śrīnivāsaḥ:** Shri here denotes men with Shri, i.e., virtue and power. He who dwells in such men is Shrinivasa.

608. **Śrīnidhiḥ:** One who is the seat of all Shri, i.e., virtues and power.

609. **Śrīvibhāvanaḥ:** One who grants every form of prosperity and virtue according to their Karma.

610. **Śrīdharaḥ:** One who bears on His chest Shri, who is the mother of all.

611. **Śrīkaraḥ:** One who makes devotees—those who praise, think about Him and worship Him—into virtuous and powerful beings.

612. **Śreyaḥ:** 'Shreyas' means the attainment of what is un-decaying good and happiness. Such a state is the nature of the Lord.

613. **Śrīmān:** One in whom there are all forms of Shri that is power, virtue, beauty, etc.

614. **Lōkatrayāśrayaḥ:** One who is the support of all the three worlds.

स्वक्षः स्वङ्गः
शतानन्दो नन्दिर्ज्योतिर्गणेश्वरः ।
विजितात्माऽविधेयात्मा
सत्कीर्तिश्छिन्नसंशयः ॥६६॥

svakṣaḥ svaṅgaḥ
śatānaṅdō naṅdirjyōtirgaṇeśvaraḥ,
vijitātmā vidheyātmā
satkīrtiśchinnasaṁśayaḥ. (66)

615. **Svakṣaḥ:** One whose Akshas (eyes) are handsome like lotus flowers.
616. **Svaṅgaḥ:** One whose limbs are beautiful.
617. **Śatānandaḥ:** One who is non-dual and is of the nature of supreme bliss.
618. **Nandiḥ:** One who is of the nature of supreme Bliss.
619. **Jyōtir-gaṇeśvaraḥ:** One who is the Lord of the stars, i.e., Jyotirgana.
620. **Vijitātmā:** One who has conquered the Atma, i.e., the mind.
621. **Vidheyātmā:** One whose form or nature cannot be determined as 'only this'.

622. **Satkīrtiḥ:** One whose fame is of the nature of truth.

623. **Chinna-saṁśayaḥ:** One who has no doubts, as everything is clear to him like a fruit in the palm.

उदीर्णः सर्वतश्चक्षुरनीशः
शाश्वतस्थिरः ।
भूशयो भूषणो
भूतिर्विशोकः शोकनाशनः ।।६७।।

udīrṇaḥ sarvataścakṣuranīśaḥ
śāśvatasthiraḥ,
bhūśayō bhūṣaṇō
bhūtirviśōkaḥ śōkanāśanaḥ. (67)

624. **Udīrṇaḥ:** He who is superior to all beings.
625. **Sarvataḥ-cakṣuḥ:** One who, being of the nature of pure consciousness, can see everthing in all directions.
626. **Anīśaḥ:** One who cannot have anyone to lord over him.
627. **Śāśvata-sthiraḥ:** One, who though eternal is also unchanging.
628. **Bhūśayaḥ:** One who, while seeking the means to cross over to Lanka, had to sleep on the ground of the sea-beach.

629. **Bhūṣaṇaḥ:** One who adorned the earth by manifesting as various incarnations.

630. **Bhūtiḥ:** One who is the abode or the essence of everthing, or is the source of all glorious manifestations.

631. **Viśōkaḥ:** One who, being of the nature of bliss, is free from all sorrow.

632. **Śōkanāśanaḥ:** One who effaces the sorrows of devotees even by mere remembrance.

अर्चिष्मानर्चितः कुम्भो
विशुद्धात्मा विशोधनः ।
अनिरुद्धोऽप्रतिरथः
प्रद्युम्नोऽमितविक्रमः ॥६८॥

arciṣmānarcitaḥ kuṁbhō
viśuddhātmā viśōdhanaḥ,
aniruddhōpratirathaḥ
pradyumnōmitavikramaḥ. (68)

633. **Arciṣmān:** He by whose rays of light (Archish), the sun, the moon and other bodies are endowed with rays of light.

634. **Arcitaḥ:** One who is worshipped by Brahma and other Devas who are themselves the objects of worship in all the worlds.

635. **Kumbhaḥ:** He who contains in Himself every thing as in a pot.

636. **Viśuddhātmā:** Being above the three Gunas, Sattva, Rajas and Tamas, the Lord is pure spirit and is also free from all impurities.

637. **Viśōdhanaḥ:** One who destroys all sins by mere remembrance.

638. **Aniruddhaḥ:** The last one of the four Vyuhas—Vasudeva, Samkarshana, Pradyumna and Aniruddhaḥ or One who cannot be obstructed by enemies.

639. **Aprati-rathaḥ:** One who has no Pratiratha or an equal antagonist to confront.

640. **Pradyumnaḥ:** One whose Dyumna or wealth is of a superior and sacred order or One of the four Vyuhas.

641. **Amitavikramaḥ:** One of unlimited prowess or One whose prowess cannot be obstructed by anyone.

कालनेमिनिहा वीरः
शौरिः शूरजनेश्वरः ।
त्रिलोकात्मा त्रिलोकेशः
केशवः केशिहा हरिः ॥६९॥

kālaneminihā vīraḥ
śauriḥ śūrajaneśvaraḥ,
trilōkātmā trilōkeśaḥ
keśavaḥ keśihā hariḥ. (69)

642. **Kālanemi-nihā:** One who destroyed the Asura named Kalanemi.
643. **Viraḥ:** One who is courageous.
644. Śauriḥ: One who was born in the clan of Sura as Krishna.
645. **Śūrajaneśvaraḥ:** One who, with his overwhelming prowess, controls great powers like Indra and others.
646. **Trilōkātmā:** One who in his capacity as the inner pervade is the soul for the three worlds.
647. **Trilōkeśaḥ:** One under whose guidance and command everything in the three words is functioning.

648. **Keśavaḥ:** By Kesha is meant the rays of light spreading within the orbit of the sun.

649. **Keśihā:** One who destroyed the Asura named Keshi.

650. **Hariḥ:** One who destroys Samsara, i.e., entanglement in the cycle of birth and death along with ignorance, its cause.

कामदेवः कामपालः
कामी कान्तः कृतागमः ।
अनिर्देश्यवपुर्विष्णुर्वीरोऽनन्तो
धनंजयः ॥७०॥

kāmadevaḥ kāmapālaḥ
kāmī kāntaḥ kṛtāgamaḥ,
anirdeśyavapurviṣṇurvīrōnantō dhanañjayaḥ. (70)

651. **Kāmadevaḥ:** One who is desired by persons in quest of the four values of life—Dharma, Artha, Kama and Moksha.

652. **Kāmapālaḥ:** One who protects or assures the desired ends of people endowed with desires.

653. **Kāmī:** One who by nature has all his desires satisfied.

654. **Kāntaḥ:** One whose form is endowed with great beauty or One who effects the Anta or dissolution of Ka or Brahma at the end of a Dviparardha (the period of Brahma's lifetime extending over a hundred divine years).

655. **Kṛtāgamaḥ:** He who produced scriptures like Shruti, Smruti and Agama.

656. **Anirdeśya-vapuḥ:** He is called so because, being above the Gunas, His form cannot be determined.

657. **Viṣṇuḥ:** One whose brilliance has spread over the sky and over the earth.

658. **Vīraḥ:** One who has the power of Gati or movement.

659. **Anantaḥ:** One who pervades everything, who is eternal, who is the soul of all, and who cannot be limited by space, time, location, etc.

660. **Dhananjayaḥ:** Arjuna is called so because by his conquest of the kingdoms in the four quarters he acquired great wealth. Arjuna is a Vibhuti, a glorious manifestation of the Lord.

ब्रह्मण्यो ब्रह्मकृद् ब्रह्मा
ब्रह्म ब्रह्मविवर्धनः ।
ब्रह्मविद् ब्राह्मणो ब्रह्मी
ब्रह्मज्ञो ब्राह्मणप्रियः ।।७१।।

brahmaṇyō brahmakṛdbrahmā
brahma brahmavivardhanaḥ,
brahmavid brāhmaṇō brahmī
brahmajñō brāhmaṇapriyaḥ. (71)

661. **Brahmaṇyaḥ:** The Vedas, Brahmanas and knowledge are indicated by the word Brahma. As the Lord promotes these, He is called Brahmanya.

662. **Brahmakṛt:** One who performs Brahma or Tapas (austerity).

663. **Brahmā:** One who creates everything as the creator Brahma.

664. **Brahma:** Being big expanding, the Lord who is known from indications like Satya (Truth), is called Brahma. Or Brahma is Truth, Knowledge and Infinity!

665. **Brahma-vivardhanaḥ:** One who promotes Tapas (austerity), etc.

666. **Brahmavid:** One who knows the Vedas and their real meaning.

667. **Brāhmaṇaḥ:** One who, in the form of Brahmana, instructs the whole world by saying, 'It is commanded so and so in the Veda.'

668. **Brahmī:** One in whom is established such entities as Tapas, Veda, mind, Prana, etc. which are parts of Brahma and which are also called Brahma.

669. **Brahmajñaḥ:** One who knows the nature of Brahman.

670. **Brāhmaṇapriyaḥ:** One to whom holy men are devoted.

महाक्रमो महाकर्मा
महातेजा महोरगः ।
महाक्रतुर्महायज्वा
महायज्ञो महाहविः ॥७२॥

mahākramō mahākarmā
mahātejā mahōragaḥ,
mahākraturmahāyajvā
mahāyajñō mahāhaviḥ. (72)

671. **Mahākramaḥ:** One with enormous strides.
672. **Mahākarmā:** One who is performing great works like the creation of the world.
673. **Mahātejāḥ:** He from whose brilliance, sun and other luminaries derive their brilliance or One who is endowed with the brilliance of various excellences.
674. **Mahoragaḥ:** The great serpent.
675. **Mahākratuḥ:** The great Kratu (sacrifice).
676. **Mahāyajvā:** One who is great and performs sacrifices for the good of the world.

677. **Mahāyajñaḥ:** He who is the great sacrifice.

678. **Mahāhaviḥ:** The great sacrificial offering, namely the world, conceived as the manifestation of Brahman.

स्तव्यः स्तवप्रियः स्तोत्रं
स्तुतिः स्तोता रणप्रियः ।
पूर्णः पूरयिता पुण्यः
पुण्यकीर्तिरनामयः ।।७३।।

stavyaḥ stavapriyaḥ stōtraṁ
stutiḥ stōtā raṇapriyaḥ,
pūrṇaḥ pūrayitā puṇyaḥ
puṇyakīrtiranāmayaḥ. (73)

679. **Stavyaḥ:** One who is the object of laudations of everyone but who never praises any other being.

680. **Stava-priyaḥ:** One who is pleased with hymns.

681. **Stotraṁ:** A Stotra means a hymn proclaiming the glory, attributes and names of the Lord.

682. **Stutiḥ:** A praise.

683. **Stōtā:** One who, being all-formed, is also the person who sings a hymn of praise.

684. **Raṇapriyaḥ:** One who is fond of fight for the protection of the world and for the purpose

always sports in His hands the five weapons—the discus Sudarshana, the mace Kaumodaki, the bow Saranga, and the sword Nandaka besides the conch Panchajanya.

685. **Pūrṇaḥ:** One who is self-fulfilled, being the source of all powers and excellences.

686. **Pūrayitā:** One who is not only self-fulfilled but gives all fulfillments to others.

687. **Puṇyaḥ:** One by only hearing about whom all sins are erased.

688. **Puṇyakīrtiḥ:** One of holy fame. His excellences are capable of conferring great merit on others.

689. **Anāmayaḥ:** One who is not afflicted by any disease that is born of cause, internal or external.

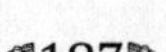

मनोजवस्तीर्थकरो
वसुरेता वसुप्रदः ।
वसुप्रदो वासुदेवो
वसुर्वसुमना हविः ॥७४॥

manōjavastīrthakarō
vasuretā vasupradaḥ,
vasupradō vāsudevō
vasurvasumanā haviḥ. (74)

690. **Manōjavaḥ:** One who, being all pervading, is said to be endowed with speed likes that of the mind.

691. **Tīrthakaraḥ:** He who renders one a purifier, enabling him to remove even others' blemishes.

692. **Vasu-retāḥ:** He whose Retas (semen) is Vasu (gold).

693. **Vasupradaḥ:** One who gladly bestows wealth in abundance. He is really the master of all wealth, and others who seem to be so are in those positions only because of His grace.

694. **Vasupradaḥ:** One who bestows on devotees the highest of all wealth, namely Moksha.

695. **Vāsudevaḥ:** The son of Vasudeva.

696. **Vasuḥ:** He in whom all creation dwells.

697. **Vasumanaḥ:** One whose mind dwells equally in all things.

698. **Haviḥ:** Havis or sacrificial offerings.

सद्गतिः सत्कृतिः सत्ता
सद्भूतिः सत्परायणः ।
शूरसेनो यदुश्रेष्ठः
सन्निवासः सुयामुनः ॥७५॥

sadgatiḥ satkṛtiḥ sattā
sadbhūtiḥ satparāyaṇaḥ,
śūrasenō yaduśreṣṭhaḥ
sannivāsaḥ suyāmunaḥ. (75)

699. **Sadgatiḥ:** One who is the refuge for truthful people or One who is endowed with intelligence of great excellence.

700. **Satkṛtiḥ:** One whose achievements are for the protection of the world.

701. **Sattā:** Experience that is without any difference of an external nature from similar objects or dissimilar objects as also internal differences is called Satta.

702. **Sad-bhūtiḥ:** The Paramatman who is pure existence and consciousness, who is unsublatable and who manifests Himself in many ways.

703. **Satparāyaṇaḥ:** He who is the highest status attainable by holy men who have realized the truth.

704. **Śūrasenaḥ:** One having an army of heroic warriors like Hanuman.

705. **Yaduśreṣṭhaḥ:** One who is the greatest among the Yadus.

706. **Sannivāsaḥ:** One who is the resort of holy knowing ones.

707. **Suyāmunaḥ:** One who is surrounded by may illustrious persons associated with the river Yamuna like Devaki, Vasudeva, Nandagopa, Yasoda, Balabhadra, Subhadra, etc.

भूतावासो वासुदेवः
सर्वासुनिलयोऽनलः ।
दर्पहा दर्पदो दृप्तो
दुर्धरोऽथापराजितः ॥७६॥

bhūtāvāsō vāsudevaḥ
sarvāsunilayōnalaḥ,
darpahā darpadō dṛptō
durdharōthāparājitaḥ. (76)

708. **Bhūtāvāsaḥ:** He in whom all the beings dwell.

709. **Vāsudevaḥ:** The Divinity who covers the whole universe by Maya.

710. **Sarvāsunilayaḥ:** He in whose form as the Jiva all the vital energy or Prana of all living beings dissolves.

711. **Analaḥ:** One whose wealth or power has no limits.

712. **Darpahā:** One who puts down the pride of persons who walk along the unrighteous path.

713. **Darpadaḥ:** One who endows those who walk the path of righteousness with a sense of self-respect regarding their way of life.

714. **Dṛptaḥ:** One who is ever satisfied by the enjoyment of His own inherent bliss.

715. **Durdharaḥ:** One who is very difficult to be borne orcontained in the heart in meditation.

716. **Aparājitaḥ:** One who is never conquered by internal enemies like attachment and by external enemies like Asuras.

विश्वमूर्तिर्महा
मूर्तिर्दीप्तमूर्तिरमूर्तिमान् ।
अनेकमूर्तिरव्यक्तः
शतमूर्तिः शताननः ।।७७।।

viśvamūrtirmahā
mūrtirdīptamūrtiramūrtimān,
anekamūrtiravyaktaḥ
śatamūrtiḥ śatānanaḥ. (77)

717. **Viśvamūrtiḥ:** One who, being the soul of all, has the whole universe as His body.

718. **Mahāmūrtiḥ:** One with an enormous form stretched on a bedstead constituted of the serpent Adisesha.

719. **Dīptamūrtiḥ:** One with a luminous form of knowledge.

720. **Amūrtimān:** He who is without a body born of Karma.

721. **Anekamūrtiḥ:** One who assumes several bodies in His incarnations as it pleases Him in or to help the world.

722. **Avyaktaḥ:** One who cannot be clearly described as 'This' even though He has many forms.

723. **Śataṃūrtiḥ:** One who, though He is of the nature of pure consciousness, assumes different forms for temporary purposes.

724. **Śatānanaḥ:** One with a hundred faces (indicating that He has several forms).

एको नैकः सवः कः किं
यत् तत्पदमनुत्तमम् ।
लोकबन्धुर्लोकनाथो
माधवो भक्तवत्सलः ।।७८।।

ekō naikaḥ savaḥ kaḥ kiṁ
yattatpadamanuttamam,
lōkabandhurlōkanāthō
mādhavō bhaktavatsalaḥ. (78)

725. **Ekaḥ:** One without any kind of differences that are internal or that relate to similar objects external or to dissimilar objects.

726. **Naikaḥ:** One who has numerous bodies born of Maya.

727. **Savaḥ:** That Yajna in which Soma is made.

728. **Kaḥ:** The syllable 'Ka' indicates joy or happiness. So it means One who is hymned as constituted of joy.

729. **Kim:** One who is fit to be contemplated upon, because He is the summation of all values.

730. **Yat:** One who is by nature existent. The word 'Yat' indicates a self-subsisting entity.

731. **Tat:** Brahma is so called because He 'expands'.

732. **Padamanuttamam:** That abode that is superlative in every way, which all seekers of Moksha aim at and reach, for redressing their needs and gaining fulfillment.

733. **Lokabandhuḥ:** One who is friend of the world.

734. **Lokanāthah:** One to whom all the worlds pray.

735. **Mādhavaḥ:** One who was born in the clan of Madhu.

736. **Bhaktavatsalaḥ:** One who has got love for devotees.

सुवर्णवर्णो हेमाङ्गो
वराङ्गश्चन्दनाङ्गदी ।
वीरहा विषमः शून्यो
घृताशीरचलश्चलः ॥७६॥

suvarṇavarṇō hemāṅgō
varāṅgaścandanāṅgadī,
vīrahā viṣamaḥ śūnyō
ghṛtāśīracalaścalaḥ. (79)

737. **Suvarṇavarṇaḥ:** One who has got the colour of gold.

738. **Hemāṅgaḥ:** One whose form is like that of gold.

739. **Varāṅgaḥ:** He the parts of whose form are brilliant.

740. **Candanāṅgadī:** One who is adorned with armlets that generate joy.

741. **Vīrahā:** One who destroyed heroes (Viras) like Kiranyakashipu for protecting Dharma.

742. **Viṣamaḥ:** One to whom there is no euql because nothing is comparable to Him by any characteristic.

743. **Śūnyaḥ:** One who, being without any attributes, appears as Sunya (empty).

744. **Ghṛtāśīḥ:** One whose blessings are unfailing.

745. **Acalaḥ:** One who cannot be deprived of His real nature as Truth, Intelligence and Infinity.

746. **Calaḥ:** One who moves in the form of air.

अमानी मानदो मान्यो
लोकस्वामी त्रिलोकधृक् ।
सुमेधा मेधजो धन्यः
सत्यमेधा धराधरः ॥८०॥

amānī mānadō mānyō
lōkasvāmī trilōkadhṛt,
sumedhā medhajō dhanyaḥ
satyamedhā dharādharaḥ. (80)

747. **Amānī:** He who, being of the nature of pure consciousness, has no sense of identification with anything that is not Atman.

748. **Mānadaḥ:** One who by His power of Maya induces the sense of self in non-self or One who has regard and beneficence towards devotees or One who destroys in the knowing ones the sense of identification with the non-self.

749. **Mānyaḥ:** One who is to be adored by all because He is the God of all.

750. **Lokasvāmī:** One who is the Lord of all the fourteen spheres.

751. **Trilokadhṛt:** One who supports all the three worlds.

752. **Sumedhāḥ:** One with great and beneficent intelligence.

753. **Medhajaḥ:** One who has arisen from Yajna (a kind of sacrifice).

754. **Dhanyaḥ:** One who has attained all His ends and, therefore, is self-satisfied.

755. **Satyamedhāḥ:** One whose intelligence is fruitful.

756. **Dharādharaḥ:** One who supports the worlds by His fractiosn like Adisesha.

तेजोवृषो द्युतिधरः
सर्वशस्त्रभृतां वरः।
प्रग्रहो निग्रहो व्यग्रो
नैकशृङ्गो गदाग्रजः ॥८१॥

tejōvr̥ṣō dyutidharaḥ
sarvaśastrabhr̥tāṁ varaḥ,
pragrahō nigrahō vyagrō
naikaśr̥ṅgō gadāgrajaḥ. (81)

757. **Tejōvr̥ṣaḥ:** One who in the form of the sun causes rainfall at all times.

758. **Dyutidharaḥ:** One whose form is always brilliant.

759. **Sarva-śastra-bhr̥tāṁ varaḥ:** One who is superior to all bearing arms.

760. **Pragrahaḥ:** One who accepts the offerings of devotees with great delight.

761. **Nigrahaḥ:** One who controls and destroys everything.

762. **Vyagraḥ:** One who has no Agra or end or One who is very attentive (Vyagra) in granting the prayers of devotees.

763. **Naikaśṛṅgaḥ:** One with four horns.

764. **Gadāgrajaḥ:** One who is revealed first by mantra (Nigada) or One who is the elder brother of Gada.

चतुर्मूर्तिश्चतुर्बाहुश्चतुर्व्यूहश्चतुर्गतिः ।
चतुरात्मा
चतुर्भावश्चतुर्वेदविदेकपात् ॥८२॥

caturmūrtiścaturbāhuścaturvyūhaścaturgatiḥ,
caturātmā
caturbhāvaścaturvedavidekapāt. (82)

765. **Caturmūrtiḥ:** One with four aspects as Virat, Sutratma, Avyakruta and Turiya or One with four horns with colours white, red, yellow and black.

766. **Caturbāhuḥ:** One with four arms, as Vasudeva is always described.

767. **Caturvyūhaḥ:** One having four manifestations.

768. **Caturgatiḥ:** One who is sought as the end by the four Orders of life and four Varnas ordained by the scriptures.

769. **Caturātmā:** One whose self is especially endowed with puissance because it is without any attachment, antagonism, etc.

770. **Caturbhāvaḥ:** One from whom has originated the four human values—Dharma, Artha, Kama and Moksha.

771. **Catur-vedavid:** One who understands the true meaning of the four Vedas.

772. **Ekapāt:** One with a single Pada, part or leg, or One with a single foot or manifestation.

समावर्तोऽनिवृत्तात्मा
दुर्जयो दुरतिक्रमः ।
दुर्लभो दुर्गमो दुर्गो
दुरावासो दुरारिहा ॥८३॥

samāvartō nivṛttātmā
durjayō duratikramaḥ,
durlabhō durgamō durgō
durāvāsō durārihā. (83)

773. **Samāvartaḥ:** One who effectively whirls the wheel of Samsara.
774. **Anivrutātmā:** One who is not Nivruta (separated from) anything or anywhere because He is all-pervading.
775. **Durjayaḥ:** One who cannot be conquered.
776. **Duratikramaḥ:** One out of fear of whom even heavenly objects like sun do not dare to oppose His command.
777. **Durlabhaḥ:** One who can be attained by Bhakti, which is difficult for a person to be endowed with.

778. **Durgamaḥ:** One who is hard to reach due to His inwardness and subtle nature.

779. **Durgaḥ:** One the attainment of whom is rendered difficult by various obstructions.

780. **Durāvāsaḥ:** He whom the Yogis with very great difficulty bring to reside in their hearts in Samadhi.

781. **Durārihā:** One who destroys beings like Asuras.

शुभाङ्गो लोकसारङ्गः
सुतन्तुस्तन्तुवर्धनः ।
इन्द्रकर्मा महाकर्मा
कृतकर्मा कृतागमः ।।८४।।

śubhāṅgō lōkasāraṅgaḥ
sutantustantuvardhanaḥ,
indrakarmā mahākarmā
kṛtakarmā kṛtāgamaḥ. (84)

782. **Śubhāṅgaḥ:** One whose form is very auspicious to meditate upon.

783. **Lōkasāraṅgaḥ:** One who like the Saranga (honey-beetle) grasps the essence of the world.

784. **Sutantuḥ:** As this universe of infinite extension belongs to Him, the Lord is called Sutantu.

785. **Tantu-vardhanaḥ:** One who can augment or contract the web of this world.

786. **Indra-karmā:** One whose actions are like that of Indra, i.e., are of a highly commendable nature.

787. **Mahākarmā:** One of whom the great elements like Akasha are effects.

788. **Kṛtakarmā:** One who has fulfilled everything and has nothing more to accomplish.

789. **Kṛtāgamaḥ:** One who has given out the Agama in the shape of the Veda.

उद्‌भवः सुन्दरः सुन्दो
रत्ननाभः सुलोचनः ।
अर्को वाजसनः श्रृंगी
जयन्तः सर्वविज्जयी ॥८५॥

udbhavaḥ sundaraḥ sundō
ratnanābhaḥ sulōcanaḥ,
arkō vājasanaḥ śṛṅgī
jayantaḥ sarvavijjayī . (85)

790. **Udbhavaḥ:** One who assumes great and noble embodiments out of His own will.
791. **Sundaraḥ:** One who has a graceful attractiveness that surprises everyone.
792. **Sundaḥ:** One who is noted for extreme tenderness (Undanam).
793. **Ratna-nābhaḥ:** Ratna indicates beauty, so One whose navel is very beautiful.
794. **Sulōcanaḥ:** One who has brilliant eyes, i.e., knowledge of everything.
795. **Arkaḥ:** One who is being worshipped even by beings like Brahma, who are themselves objects of worship.

796. **Vājasanaḥ:** One who gives Vajam (food) to those who entreat Him.

797. **Śṛṅgī:** One who at the time of Pralaya assumed the form of a fish having prominent antenna.

798. **Jayantaḥ:** One who conquers enemies easily.

799. **Sarvavijjayī:** The Lord is Sarvavit as He has knowledge of everything. He is Jayi because He is the conqueror of all the inner forces like attachment, anger, etc., as also of external foes like Hiranyaksha.

सुवर्णबिन्दुरक्षोभ्यः
सर्ववागीश्वरेश्वरः ।
महाह्रदो महागर्तो
महाभूतो महानिधिः ॥८६॥

suvarṇabindurakṣōbhyaḥ
sarvavāgīśvareśvaraḥ,
mahāhradō mahāgartō
mahābhūtō mahānidhiḥ. (86)

800. **Suvarṇabinduḥ:** One whose Bindus, i.e., limbs, are equal to gold in brilliance.

801. **Akṣobhyaḥ:** One who is never perturbed by passions like attachment and aversion, by objects of the senses like sound, taste, etc., and by Asuras the antagonists of the Devas.

802. **Sarva-vāgīśvareśvaraḥ:** One who is the master of all masters of learning, including Brahma.

803. **Mahāhradaḥ:** He is called a great Hrada (lake) because being the Paramatman who is of the nature of Bliss, the Yogis who

contemplate upon Him dip themselves in that lake of Bliss and attain to great joy.

804. **Mahāgartaḥ:** One whose Maya is difficult to cross like a big pit.

805. **Mahābhūtaḥ:** One who is not divided by the three periods of time—past, present and future.

806. **Mahānidhiḥ:** One in whom all the great elements have their support. He is Mahan or the great one, and Nidhi, the most precious one.

कुमुदः कुन्दरः कुन्दः
पर्जन्यः पावनोऽनिलः ।
अमृताशोऽमृतवपुः
सर्वज्ञः सर्वतोमुखः ॥८७॥

kumudaḥ kundaraḥ kundaḥ
parjanyaḥ pāvano'nilaḥ,
amṛtāśōmṛtavapuḥ
sarvajñaḥ sarvatōmukhaḥ. (87)

807. **Kumudaḥ:** One who gives Muda (joy) to the earth by freeing it of its burdens.

808. **Kundaraḥ:** One who offers blessings as pure as Kunda or jasmine.

809. **Kundaḥ:** One who has limbs as beautiful as Kunda or jasmine.

810. **Parjanyaḥ:** One who, like clouds, redresses the heat of the threefold sufferings (psycho-intellectual, material and Providential), and also sheds like rain the objects of desire.

811. **Pāvanaḥ:** One by merely remembering whom a devotee attains purity.

812. **Anilaḥ:** 'Ilanam' means inducement. One who is without any inducement is Anila. 'Ilana' also means sleep. So, One who sleeps not or is ever awake is Anila.

813. **Amṛtāśaḥ:** One who consumes Amruta or immortal bliss, which is His own nature.

814. **Amṛtavapuḥ:** One whose form is deathless, i.e., undecaying.

815. **Sarvajñaḥ:** One who is all-knowing.

816. **Sarvatōmukhaḥ:** One who has faces everywhere.

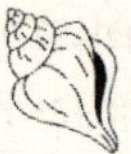

सुलभः सुव्रतः सिद्धः शत्रुजिच्छत्रुतापनः ।
न्यग्रोधोऽदुम्बरोऽश्वत्थश्चाणूरान्ध्रनिषूदनः ॥८८॥

sulabhaḥ suvrataḥ siddhaḥ
śatrujicchatrutāpanaḥ,
nyagrodho'dumbaro'śvatthaś
cāṇūrāndhraniṣūdanaḥ. (88)

817. **Sulabhaḥ:** One who is attained easily by offering trifles like leaf, flower, fruits, etc., with devotion.

818. **Suvrataḥ:** 'Vratati' means to enjoy, so 'Suvratah' means One who enjoys pure offerings. It can also mean One who is a non-enjoyer, i.e., a mere witness.

819. **Siddhaḥ:** One whose objects are always attained, i.e., omnipotent and unobstructed by any other will.

820. **Śatrujit:** Conqueror of all forces of evil.

821. **Śatrutāpanaḥ:** One who destroys the enemies of the Devas.

822. **Nyagrodhaḥ:** That which remains above all and grows downward, i.e., He is the source of everything that is manifest.

823. **Udumbaraḥ:** One who, as the supreme cause, is 'above the sky', i.e., superior to all.

824. **Aśvatthaḥ:** That which does not last even till the next day.

825. **Cāṇūrāndhra-niṣūdanaḥ:** One who destroyed the valiant fighter Chanura belonging to the race of Andhra.

सहस्रार्चिः सप्तजिह्वः
सप्तैधाः सप्तवाहनः ।
अमूर्तिरनघोऽचिन्त्यो
भयकृद्भयनाशनः ॥८९॥

sahasrārciḥ saptajihvaḥ
saptaidhāḥ saptavāhanaḥ,
amūrtiranaghōcintyō
bhayakṛdbhayanāśanaḥ. (89)

826. **Sahasrārciḥ:** One with innumerable Archis or rays.

827. **Sapta-jihvaḥ:** The Lord in his manifestation as Fire is conceived as having seven tongues of flame.

828. **Saptaidhāḥ:** The Lord who is of the nature of fire has seven Edhas or forms of brilliance.

829. **Saptavāhanaḥ:** The Lord in the form of Surya or sun has seven horses as his vehicles or mounts.

830. **Amūrtiḥ:** One who is without sins or without sorrow.

831. **Achintyo:** One who is not determinable by any criteria of knowledge.

832. **Anaghaḥ:** One who is without sins or without sorrow.

833. **Bhayakṛud:** One who generates fear in those who go along the evil path or One who cuts at the root of all fear.

834. **Bhaya-nāśanaḥ:** One who destroys the fears of the virtuous.

अणुर्बृहत्कृशः स्थूलो
गुणभृन्निर्गुणो महान् ।
अधृतः स्वधृतः स्वास्यः
प्राग्वंशो वंशवर्धनः ॥९०॥

aṇurbṛhatkṛśaḥ sthūlō
guṇabhṛnnirguṇō mahān,
adhṛtassvadhṛtasvāsyaḥ
prāgvaṁśō vaṁśavardhanaḥ. (90)

835. **Aṇuḥ:** One who is extremely subtle.
836. **Bṛhat:** The huge and mighty.
837. **Kṛśaḥ:** One who is non-material.
838. **Sthūlaḥ:** Being the inner pervader of all, He is figuratively described as Stula or huge.
839. **Guṇa-bhṛt:** The support of the Gunas. He is called so because in the creative cycle of creation, sustenance and dissolution, He is the support of the Gunas—Sattva, Rajas and Tamas—with which these functions are performed.
840. **Nirguṇaḥ:** One who is without the Gunas of Prakruti.

841. **Mahān:** The great.

842. **Adhṛutaḥ:** One who, being the support of all supporting agencies, like Pruthvi (earth), is not supported by anything external to Him.

843. **Svadhṛtaḥ:** One supported by Oneself.

844. **Svāsyaḥ:** One whose face is beautiful and slightly red like the inside of a lotus flower.

845. **Prāgvaṁśaḥ:** The family lines of others are preceded by the lines of still others, but the Lord's descendent, namely, the world system, is not preceded by anything else.

846. **Vaṁśavardhanaḥ:** One who augments or destroys the world-system, which is His off-spring.

भारभृत् कथितो योगी
योगीशः सर्वकामदः ।
आश्रमः श्रमणः क्षामः
सुपर्णो वायुवाहनः ॥९१॥

bhārabhṛt kathitō yōgī
yōgīśaḥ sarvakāmadaḥ,
āśramaḥ śramaṇaḥ kṣāmaḥ
suparṇō vāyuvāhanaḥ. (91)

847. **Bhārabhṛt:** One who bears the weight of the earth assuming the form of Ananta.

848. **Kathitaḥ:** One who is spoken of as the highest by the Veda or One of whom all Vedas speak.

849. **Yogī:** He who is always fused into and united with Himself, His creation and manifestation, and hence remains a Yogi ceaselessly.

850. **Yogīśaḥ:** He who is never shaken from Yoga or knowledge and establishment in His own self, unlike ordinary Yogis who slip away from Yoga on account of obstacles.

851. **Sarva-kāmadaḥ:** One who bestows all desired fruits.

852. **Āśramaḥ:** One who is the bestower of rest on all who are wandering in the forest of Samsara.

853. **Śramaṇaḥ:** One who brings tribulations to those who live without using their discriminative power.

854. **Kṣāmaḥ:** He who brings about the decline of all beings.

855. **Suparṇaḥ:** The lord who has manifested Himself as the tree of Samsara has excellent leaves (Parna) in the form of Vedic passages (Chandas).

856. **Vāyuvāhanaḥ:** He for fear of whom Vayu carries all beings.

धनुर्धरो धनुर्वेदो
दण्डो दमयिता दमः ।
अपराजितः सर्वसहो
नियन्ताऽनियमोऽयमः ॥९२॥

dhanurdharō dhanurvedō
daṅḍō damayitā damaḥ,
aparājitassarvasahō
niyantā niyamō yamaḥ. (92)

857. **Dhanurdharaḥ:** He who as Rama wielded the great bow.

858. **Dhanurvedaḥ:** He who, as the same Rama, the son of Dasharatha, was the master of the science of archery.

859. **Daṅḍaḥ:** He who is discipline among the disciplinarians.

860. **Damayitā:** He who inflicts punishments on people as Yama and as king.

861. **Damaḥ:** He who is in the form of self-discipline in men as a result of enforcement.

862. **Aparājitaḥ:** One who is never defeated by enemies.

863. **Sarvasahaḥ:** One who is expert in all Karma.

864. **Niyantā:** One who appoints every person to his respective duties.

865. **Aniyamaḥ:** One on whom there is no enforcement of any law, or above whom there can be no overlord to enforce anything, as He is the controller of everything.

866. **Ayamaḥ:** One on whom Yama has no control, i.e., One who has no death.

सत्त्ववान् सात्त्विकः सत्यः
सत्यधर्मपरायणः ।
अभिप्रायः प्रियार्होऽर्हः
प्रियकृत् प्रीतिवर्धनः ॥९३॥

sattvavān sāttvikaḥ satyaḥ
satyadharmaparāyaṇaḥ,
abhiprāyaḥ priyārho'rhaḥ
priyakṛt pritivardhanaḥ. (93)

867. **Sattvavān:** One who has the strengthening qualities like heroism, prowess, etc.

868. **Sāttvikaḥ:** One who is established essentially in the Sattva Guna.

869. **Satyaḥ:** One who is truly established in good people.

870. **Satya-dharma-parāyaṇaḥ:** One who is present in truthfulness and righteousness in its many aspects.

871. **Abhiprāyaḥ:** One who is sought after by those who seek the ultimate values of life (Purushartha).

872. **Priyārhaḥ:** The being to whom the objects

that are dear to oneself, are fit to be offered.

873. **Arhaḥ:** One who deserves to be worshipped with all the ingredients and rites of worship like offerings, praise, prostration, etc.

874. **Priyakṛt:** One who is not only to be loved but who does what is good and dear to those who worship Him.

875. **Pritivardhanaḥ:** One who enhances the joys of devotees.

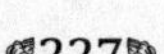

विहायसगतिर्ज्योतिः
सुरुचिर्हुतभुग्विभुः ।
रविर्विरोचनः सूर्यः
सविता रविलोचनः ।।९४।।

vihāyasagatirjyōtiḥ
surucirhutabhugvibhuḥ,
ravirvirōcanaḥ sūryaḥ
savitā ravilōcanaḥ. (94)

876. **Vihāyasa-gatiḥ:** One who is the support of Vishupada.

877. **Jyotiḥ:** One who is the light of self-luminous consciousness that reveals oneself as well as other things.

878. **Suruciḥ:** The Lord whose Ruchi, i.e., brilliance or will, is of an attractive nature.

879. **Hutabhuk:** One who eats, i.e., receives, whatever is offered to whatever deities (Devas) in all sacrifices.

880. **Vibhuḥ:** One who dwells everywhere or One who is the master of all the three worlds.

881. **Raviḥ:** One who absorbs all Rasas (fluids) in the form of the sun.

882. **Virōcanaḥ:** One who shines in many ways.

883. **Sūryaḥ:** One who generates Shri or brilliance in Surya.

884. **Savitā:** One who brings forth (Prasava) all the worlds.

885. **Ravi-lōcanaḥ:** One having the sun as the eye.

अनन्तो हुतभुग्भोक्ता
सुखदो नैकजोऽग्रजः ।
अनिर्विण्णः सदामर्षी
लोकाधिष्ठानमद्भुतः ॥९५॥

anantō hutabhugbhōktā
sukhadō naikajōgrajaḥ,
anirviṇṇaḥ sadāmarṣī
lōkādhiṣṭhānamadbhutaḥ. (95)

886. **Anantaḥ:** One who is eternal, all-pervading and indeterminable by space and time.

887. **Hutabhuk:** One who consumes what is offered in fire sacrifices.

888. **Bhoktā:** One to whom the unconscious Prakruti is the object for enjoyment.

889. **Sukhadaḥ:** One who bestows liberation (Miksha) on devotees.

890. **Naikajaḥ:** One who takes on birth again and again for the preservation of Dharma.

891. **Agrajaḥ:** One who was born before everything else, i.e., Hiranyagarbha.

892. **Anirviṇṇaḥ:** One who is free from all sorrow, because he has secured all his desires and has no obstruction in the way of such achievement.

893. **Sadāmarṣī:** One who is always patient towards good men.

894. **Lōkādhiṣṭhānam:** Brahman who, though without any other support for Himself, supports all the three worlds.

895. **Adbhutaḥ:** The wonderful being.

सनात्सनातनतमः
कपिलः कपिरव्ययः ।
स्वस्तिदः स्वस्तिकृत्स्वस्ति
स्वस्तिभुक्स्वस्तिदक्षिणः ॥९६॥

sanātsanātanatamaḥ
kapilaḥ kapiravyayaḥ,
svastidaḥ svastikṛtsvasti
svastibhuksvastidakṣiṇaḥ. (96)

896. **Sanāt:** The word Sanat indicates a great length of time. Time also is the manifestation of the Supreme Being.

897. **Sanātanatamaḥ:** Being the cause of all, He is more ancient than Brahma and other beings, who are generally considered eternal.

898. **Kapilaḥ:** A subterranean fire in the ocean is Kapila, light red in colour.

899. **Kapiḥ:** 'Ka' means water. One who drinks or absorbs all water by his Kapi, i.e., the sun.

900. **Avyayaḥ:** One in whom all the worlds get dissolved in Pralaya.

901. **Svastidaḥ:** One who gives what is auspicious to devotees.

902. **Svastikṛt:** One who works bestowing what is good.

903. **Svasti:** One whose auspicious form is characterized by supreme Bliss.

904. **Svastibhuk:** One who enjoys the Svasti (auspiciousness) mentioned above or who preserves the Svasti of devotees.

905. **Svastidakṣiṇaḥ:** One who augments as Svasti.

अरौद्रः कुण्डली चक्री
विक्रम्यूर्जितशासनः ।
शब्दातिगः शब्दसहः
शिशिरः शर्वरीकरः ।।९७।।

araudraḥ kuṇḍalī cakrī vikramyūrjitaśāsanaḥ,
śabdātigaḥ śabdasahaḥ
śiśiraḥ śarvarīkaraḥ. (97)

906. **Araudraḥ:** Action, attachment and anger these three are Raudra. The Lord is One whose desires are all accomplished, so He has no attachment or aversion. He is free from the Raudras mentioned above.

907. **Kuṇḍalī:** One who has taken the form of Adisesha.

908. **Cakrī:** One who sports in his hand the discus named Sudarshana, which is the category known as Manas, for the protection of all the worlds.

909. **Vikramī:** One who takes a stride; Courageous.

910. **Ūrjita-śāsanaḥ:** One whose dictates in the form of Shrutis and Smrutis are of an extremely sublime nature.

911. **Śabdātigaḥ:** One who cannot be denoted by any sound because He has none of the characteristics that can be grasped by sound.

912. **Śabdasahaḥ:** One who is the purport of all Vedas.

913. **Śiśiraḥ:** One who is the shelter to those who are bruning in the three types of wordly fires—sufferings arising from material causes, psychological causes and spiritual causes.

914. **Śarvarīkaraḥ:** For those in bondage, the Atman is like Sarvari (night) and for an enlightened one the state of samsara is like night (Sarvari). So, the Lord is called One who generates Sarvari or night for both the enlightened and the bound ones.

अक्रूरः पेशलो दक्षो
दक्षिणः क्षमिणांवरः ।
विद्वत्तमो वीतभयः
पुण्यश्रवणकीर्तनः ॥९८॥

akrūraḥ peśalō dakṣō
dakṣiṇaḥ, kṣamiṇāṁ varaḥ,
vidvattamō vītabhayaḥ
puṇyaśravaṇakīrtanaḥ. (98)

915. **Akrūraḥ:** One who is without cruelty.

916. **Peśalaḥ:** One who is handsome with regard to His actions, mind, word and body.

917. **Dakṣaḥ:** One who is full-grown and strong, and does every thing quickly.

918. **Dakṣiṇaḥ:** One who is effective in gaining whatever he aims for.

919. **Kṣamiṇāṁ varaḥ:** The greatest among the patient ones because He is more patient than all Yogis noted for patience.

920. **Vidvattamaḥ:** He who has the unsurpassable and all-inclusive knowledge of everything.

921. **Vītabhayaḥ:** One who, being eternally free and the Lord of all, is free from the fear of trnsmigratory life.

922. **Puṇya-śravaṇa-kīrtanaḥ:** One to hear about whom and to sing of whom is meritorious.

उत्तारणो दुष्कृतिहा
पुण्यो दुःस्वप्ननाशनः ।
वीरहा रक्षणः सन्तो
जीवनः पर्यवस्थितः ॥९९॥

uttāraṇō duṣkṛtihā
puṇyō duḥsvapnanāśanaḥ,
vīrahā rakṣaṇassantō
jīvanaḥ paryavasthitaḥ. (99)

923. **Uttāraṇaḥ:** One who takes beings over to the other shore of the ocean of Samsara.

924. **Duṣkṛtihā:** One who effaces the evil effects of evil actions or One who destroys those who perform evil.

925. **Puṇyaḥ:** One who bestows holiness on those who remember and adore Him.

926. **Duḥsvapna-nāśanaḥ:** When adored and meditated upon, He saves one from dreams foreboding danger. Hence, He is called so.

927. **Vīrahā:** One who frees Jivas from bondage and thus saves them from the various transmigratory paths by bestowing liberation on them.

928. **Rakṣaṇaḥ:** One who, assuming the Sattvaguna, protects all the three worlds.

929. **Santaḥ:** Those who adopt the virtuous path are called Santah (good men).

930. **Jīvanaḥ:** One who supports the lives of all beings as Prana.

931. **Paryavasthitaḥ:** One who remains pervading everywhere in this universe.

अनन्तरूपोऽनन्त
श्रीर्जितमन्युर्भयापहः ।
चतुरश्रो गभीरात्मा
विदिशो व्यादिशो दिशः ॥१००॥

anantarūpōnanta
śrīrjitamanyurbhayāpahaḥ,
caturaśrō gabhīrātmā
vidiśō vyādiśō diśaḥ. (100)

932. **Ananta-rūpaḥ:** One who has innumerable forms, as He dwells in this all-comprehending universe.

933. **Anantaśrīḥ:** One whose Shri (glory) is infinite.

934. **Jita-manyuḥ:** One who has overcome anger.

935. **Bhayāpahaḥ:** One who destroys the fears of beings from Samsara.

936. **Caturaśraḥ:** One who is just because He bestows on Jivas the fruits of their Karma.

937. **Gabhirātmā:** One whose nature is unfathomable.

938. **Vidiśaḥ:** One who distributes various furits of actions to persons differing in their forms according to competency.

939. **Vyādiśaḥ:** One who gives to Indra and other deities directions according to their varied functions.

940. **Diśaḥ:** One who in the form of the Vedas bestows the fruits of their ritualistic actions on different beings.

अनादिर्भूर्भुवो लक्ष्मीः
सुवीरो रुचिराङ्गदः ।
जननो जनजन्मादिर्भीमो
भीमपराक्रमः ॥१०१॥

anādirbhūrbhuvō lakṣmī
ssuvīrō rucirāṅgadaḥ,
janaṅō janajanmādirbhīmō
bhīmaparākramaḥ. (101)

941. **Anādiḥ:** One who has no beginning because He is the ultimate cause of all.

942. **Bhūrbhuvaḥ:** 'Bhu' means support. One who is the Bhu of even the earth, which is known to support all things.

943. **Lakṣmiḥ:** He who is the bestower of all that is auspicious to the earth besides being its supporter.

944. **Suvīraḥ:** One who has many brilliant ways of manifestation.

945. **Ruchirāṅgadaḥ:** One who has very attractive armlets.

946. **Jananaḥ:** One who gives birth to living beings.

947. **Jana-janmādiḥ:** One who is the root cause of the origin of Jivas that come to have embodiment.

948. **Bhimaḥ:** One who is the cause of fear.

949. **Bhima-parākramaḥ:** One whose power and courage in His incarnations were a cause of fear for the Asuras.

आधारनिलयोऽधाता
पुष्पहासः प्रजागरः ।
ऊर्ध्वगः सत्पथाचारः
प्राणदः प्रणवः पणः ।।१०२।।

ādhāranilayōdhātā
puṣpahāsaḥ prajāgaraḥ,
ūrdhvagassatpathācāraḥ
prāṇadaḥ praṇavaḥ paṇaḥ. (102)

950. **Ādhāra-nilayaḥ:** One who is the support of even all the basic supporting factors like the five elements—Ether, Air, Fire, Water and Earth.

951. **Adhātā:** One who is one's own support and, therefore, does not require another support.

952. **Puṣpahāsaḥ:** One whose manifestation as the universe resembles the Hasa or blooming of buds into flowers.

953. **Prajāgaraḥ:** One who is particularly awake, because He is eternal Awareness.

954. **Ūrdhvagaḥ:** One who is above everything.

955. **Satpathācāraḥ:** One who follows the conduct of the good.

956. **Prāṇadaḥ:** One who givesback life to dead ones as in the case of Parikshit.

957. **Praṇavaḥ:** One who, as Om, the sound symbol, is inextricably linked to Brahman.

958. **Paṇaḥ:** It comes from the root Prana, meaning transaction. So, One who bestows the fruits of Karma on all according to their Karma.

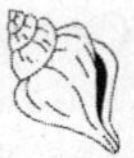

प्रमाणं प्राणनिलयः
प्राणभृत्प्राणजीवनः ।
तत्त्वं तत्त्वविदेकात्मा
जन्ममृत्युजरातिगः ।।१०३।।

pramāṇaṁ prāṇanilayaḥ
prāṇabhṛt prāṇajīvanaḥ,
tattvaṁ tattvavidekātmā
janmamṛtyujarātigaḥ. (103)

959. **Pramāṇaṁ:** One who is self-certifying as He is pure consciousness.
960. **Prāṇanilayaḥ:** The home or dissolving ground of the Pranas.
961. **Prāṇa-bhṛt:** One who strengthens the Pranas as Anna.
962. **Prāṇa-jīvanaḥ:** He who keeps alive human beings with Vayus (airs) known as Prana, Apana, etc.
963. **Tattvaṁ:** One who is the presence denoted by the word 'Tat', namely, Satyam (truth), Amritam (the immortal), Paramaartham (supreme reality), etc. These are not matter or energy.

964. **Tatvavid:** One who knowns His own true nature.

965. **Ekātmā:** One who is the sole being and the spirit (Atma) in all.

966. **Janma-mṛtyu-jarātigaḥ:** One who subsists without being subject to the six kinds of transformations—being born, existing, temporarily, growing, transforming, decaying and dying.

भूर्भुवःस्वस्तरुस्तारः
सविता प्रपितामहः ।
यज्ञो यज्ञपतिर्यज्वा
यज्ञाङ्गो यज्ञवाहनः ॥१०४॥

bhūrbhuvaḥsvastarustāraḥ
savitā prapitāmahaḥ,
yajñō yajñapatiryajvā
yajñāṅgō yajñavāhanaḥ. (104)

967. **Bhūr-bhuvaḥ-svastaruḥ:** The three Vyahrutis, Bhuh, Bhuvah, Svah, are said to be the essence of Veda.

968. **Tāraḥ:** One who helps Jivas to go across the ocean of Samsara.

969. **Savitā:** He who generates all the worlds.

970. **Prapitāmahaḥ:** One who is the father of Brahma and, therefore, the grandfather of all.

971. **Yajñaḥ:** One who is of the form of Yajna.

972. **Yajñapatiḥ:** One who is the protector and the master of the Yajnas.

973. **Yajvā:** One who manifests as the performer of a Yajna.

974. **Yajñāngaḥ:** All the parts of His body as the incarnate Cosmic Boar are identified with the parts of a Yajna.

975. **Yajña-vāhanaḥ:** One who supports the Yajna that yields various fruits.

यज्ञभृद् यज्ञकृद् यज्ञी
यज्ञभुग् यज्ञसाधनः ।
यज्ञान्तकृद् यज्ञगुह्यमन्नमन्नाद
एव च ॥१०५॥

yajñabhṛdyajñakṛdyajñī
yajñabhugyajñasādhanaḥ,
yajñāntakṛd yajñaguhyamannamannāda
eva ca. (105)

976. **Yajñabhṛd:** He is called so because He is the protector and supporter of all Yajna.
977. **Yajñakṛd:** One who performs Yajna at the beginnig and end of the world.
978. **Yajñi:** One who is the Principal.
979. **Yajñabhug:** One who is the enjoyer of Yajna or Protector of Yajna.
980. **Yajña-sādhanaḥ:** One to whom Yajna is the approach.
981. **Yajñāntakṛd:** One who is the end or the fruits of Yajna.

982. **Yayajñaguhyam:** The Gyana Yajna or the sacrifice of knowledge, which is the esoteric (Guhyam) of all the Yajnams.

983. **Annam:** That which is eaten by living beings or He who eats all beings.

984. **Annādaḥ:** One who is the eater of the whole world as food. The word 'Eva' is added to show that He is also Anna, the food eaten.

आत्मयोनिः स्वयञ्जातो
वैखानः सामगायनः ।
देवकीनन्दनः स्रष्टा
क्षितीशः पापनाशनः ॥१०६॥

ātmayōniḥ svayaṁjātō
vaikhānaḥ sāmagāyanaḥ,
devakīnandanaḥ sraṣṭā
kṣitīśaḥ pāpanāśanaḥ. (106)

985. **Ātmayōniḥ:** One who is the source of all, i.e., there is no material cause other than Himself for the universe.
986. **Svayaṁ-jātaḥ:** He is also the instrumental cause.
987. **Vaikhānaḥ:** One who excavated the earth, taking a unique form.
988. **Sāmagāyanaḥ:** One who recites the Sama chants.
989. **Devakī-nandanaḥ:** The Son of Devaki in the incarnation as Krishna.
990. **Sraṣṭā:** The creator of all the worlds.

991. **Kṣitīśaḥ:** A master of the world. Here it denotes Rama.

992. **Pāpanāśanaḥ:** He who destroys the sins of those who adore Him, meditate upon Him, remember and sing hymns of praise on Him.

शङ्खभृन्नन्दकी चक्री
शार्ङ्गधन्वा गदाधरः ।
रथाङ्गपाणिरक्षोभ्यः
सर्वप्रहरणायुधः ॥१०७॥

सर्वप्रहरणायुध ॐ नम इति ।

śaṅkhabhṛnnandakī cakrī
śārṅgadhanvā gadādharaḥ,
rathāṅgapāṇirakṣōbhyaḥ
sarvapraharaṇāyudhaḥ. (107)

sarvapraharaṇāyudha oṃ nama iti.

993. **Śaṅkhabhṛt:** One who sports the conch known as Panchajanya, which stands for Tamasahamkara, of which the five elements are born.

994. **Nandakī:** One who has in His hand the sword known as Nandaka, which stands for Vidya (spiritual illumination).

995. **Cakri:** One who sports the discus known as Sudarshana.

996. **Śārṅga-dhanvā:** One who aims His Sarnga bow.

997. Gadādharaḥ: One who has the mace known as the Kaumodaki, which stands for the category of Buddhi.

998. **Rathāṅga-pāṇiḥ:** One in whose hand is a Chakra (wheel).

999. **Akṣobhyaḥ:** One who cannot be upset by anything, because He controls all the above-mentioned weapons.

1000. **Sarva-praharaṇā-yudhaḥ:** There is no rule that the Lord has got only the above-mentioned weapons. All things, which can be used for contacting or striking, are His weapons.

Chant this shloka three times

वनमाली गदी शार्ङ्गी
शङ्खी चक्री च नन्दकी ।
श्रीमान् नारायणो
विष्णुर्वासुदेवोऽभिरक्षतु ।।१०८।।

श्री वासुदेवोऽभिरक्षतु ॐ नम इति ।

vanamālī gadī śārṅgī
śaṅkhī cakrī ca nandakī,
śrīmān nārāyaṇō
viṣṇurvāsudevōbhirakṣatu. (108)

śrī vāsudevo'bhirakṣatu oṃ nama iti.

Protect us Oh Lord Narayana, Who wears the forest garland, Who has the mace, conch, sword and the wheel, and Who is called Vishnu and the Vasudeva.

Phalashruthi

उत्तरन्यासः

- भीष्म उवाच -

इतीदं कीर्तनीयस्य
केशवस्य महात्मनः ।
नाम्नां सहस्रं
दिव्यानामशेषेण प्रकीर्तितम् ॥१॥

uttaranyāsaḥ

- bhīṣma uvāca -

itīdaṁ kīrtanīyasya
keśavasya mahātmanaḥ,
nāmnāṁ sahasraṁ
divyānāmaśeṣeṇa prakīrtitam (1)

- Bhishma said -

Thus were told all the holy thousand names of Kesava, who is great.

य इदं शृणुयान्नित्यं
यश्चापि परिकीर्तयेत् ।
नाशुभं प्राप्नुयात्किञ्चित्सोऽमुत्रेह
च मानवः ॥२॥

ya idaṁ śṛṇuyānnityaṁ yaścāpi parikīrtayet,
nāśubhaṁ prāpnuyāt kiñcit sōmutreha
ca mānavaḥ. (2)

He who hears this daily and whoever recites it shall not attain to any evil, he shall be protected in this world and in the next.

वेदान्तगो ब्राह्मणः
स्यात्क्षत्रियो विजयी भवेत् ।
वैश्यो धनसमृद्धः
स्याच्छूद्रः सुखमवाप्नुयात् ।।३।।

vedāntagō brāhmaṇaḥ
syāt kṣatriyō vijayī bhavet,
vaiśyo dhanasamṛddhaḥ
syācchūdraḥ sukhamavāpnuyāt. (3)

The Brahmin will get knowledge, the Kshatriya will get victory, the Vaisya will get wealth, the Shudra will get pleasure by reading these.

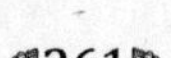

धर्मार्थी प्राप्नुयाद्धर्ममर्थार्थी
चार्थमाप्नुयात् ।
कामानवाप्नुयात्कामी
प्रजार्थी प्राप्नुयात्प्रजाम् ।।४।।

dharmārthī prāpnuyāddharmamarthārthī
cārthamāpnuyāt.
kāmānavāpnuyātkāmī
prajārthī prāpnuyātprajām. (4)

He who seeks righteousness obtains righteousness, and he who seeks wealth obtains wealth. He who seeks progeny obtains his desires.

भक्तिमान् यः सदोत्थाय
शुचिस्तद्गतमानसः ।
सहस्रं वासुदेवस्य
नाम्नामेतत्प्रकीर्तयेत् ।।५।।

bhaktimān yaḥ sadōtthāya
śucistadgatamānasaḥ,
sahasraṁ vāsudevasya
nāmnāmetat rakīrtayet. (5)

Whichever devoted man, getting up early in the morning and purifying himself, repeats this hymn devoted to Vasudeva, with a mind that is concentrated on Him...

यशः प्राप्नोति विपुलं
ज्ञातिप्राधान्यमेव च ।
अचलां श्रियमाप्नोति
श्रेयः प्राप्नोत्यनुत्तमम् ।।६।।

yaśaḥ prāpnōti vipulaṁ
yāti prādhānyameva ca,
acalāṁ śriyamāpnōti
śreyaḥ prāpnōtyanuttamam. (6)

... That man attains to great fame, leadership among his peers, wealth that is secure and the supreme good unsupassed by anything...

न भयं क्वचिदाप्नोति
वीर्यं तेजश्च विन्दति ।
भवत्यरोगो
द्युतिमान्बलरूपगुणान्वितः ।।७।।

na bhayaṁ kvacidāpnōti
vīryaṁ tejaśca viṁdati,
bhavatyarogo
dyutimānbalarūpaguṇānvitaḥ. (7)

He will be free from all fears and be endowed with great courage and energy, and he will be free from diseases.

रोगार्तो मुच्यते रोगाद्बद्धो
मुच्येत बन्धनात् ।
भयान्मुच्येत भीतस्तु
मुच्येतापन्न आपदः ।।८।।

rōgārtō mucyate rōgādbaddhō
mucyeta bandhanāt,
bhayānmucyeta bhītastu
mucyetāpanna āpadaḥ. (8)

Beauty of form, strength of body and mind, and virtuous character will be natural to him.

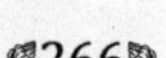

दुर्गाण्यतितरत्याशु
पुरुषः पुरुषोत्तमम् ।
स्तुवन्नामसहस्रेण
नित्यं भक्तिसमन्वितः ॥९॥

durgāṇyatitaratyāśu
puruṣaḥ puruṣōttamam,
stuvannāmasahasreṇa
nityaṁ bhaktisamanvitaḥ. (9)

A man quickly crosses over difficulties by praising the Supreme Person with a thousand names, ever accompanied by devotion.

वासुदेवाश्रयो मर्त्यो
वासुदेवपरायणः ।
सर्वपापविशुद्धात्मा याति
ब्रह्म सनातनम् ।।१०।।

vāsudevāśrayō martyō
vāsudevaparāyaṇaḥ,
sarvapāpaviśuddhātmā yāti
brahma sanātanam. (10)

A mortal who takes refuge in Vasudeva and is devoted to Vasudeva, purified of all sins, attains to the eternal Brahman.

न वासुदेवभक्तानामशुभं
विद्यते क्वचित् ।
जन्ममृत्युजराव्याधिभयं
नैवोपजायते ॥११॥

na vāsudevabhaktānāmaśubhaṁ
vidyate kvacit,
janmamṛtyujaravyādhibhayaṁ
naivōpajāyate. (11)

There is nothing inauspicious for the devotees of Vasudeva. They are not afraid of birth, death, old age or disease.

इमं स्तवमधीयानः
श्रद्धाभक्तिसमन्वितः ।
युज्येतात्मसुखक्षान्ति
श्रीधृतिस्मृतिकीर्तिभिः ॥१२॥

imaṁ stavamadhīyānaḥ
śraddhābhaktisamanvitaḥ,
yujyetātmāsukhakṣāmti
śrīdhṛtismṛtikīrtibhiḥ. (12)

One who studies this hymn with faith and devotion will be endowed with happiness, forbearance, prosperity, patience, memory and fame.

न क्रोधो न च मात्सर्यं न
लोभो नाशुभा मतिः ।
भवन्ति कृत पुण्यानां
भक्तानां पुरुषोत्तमे ।।१३।।

na krōdhō na ca mātsaryaṁ na
lōbhō nāśubhā matiḥ,
bhavantl kṛtapuṇyanaṁ
bhaktānāṁ puruṣōttame. (13)

The devotee of Lord Purushottama has neither anger nor fear, nor avarice and nor bad thoughts.

द्यौः सचन्द्रार्कनक्षत्रा
खं दिशो भूर्महोदधिः ।
वासुदेवस्य वीर्येण
विधृतानि महात्मनः ।।१४।।

dyaussacandrārkanakṣatrā
khaṁ diśō bhūrmahōdadhiḥ,
vāsudevasya vīryeṇa
vidhṛtāni mahātmanaḥ. (14)

The heavens, the moon, the sun, the stars, the sky, the directions, the earth and the ocean are sustained by the might of the great soul Vasudeva.

ससुरासुरगन्धर्वं
सयक्षोरगराक्षसम् ।
जगद्वशे वर्ततेदं
कृष्णस्य सचराचरम् ।।१५।।

sasurāsuragandharvaṁ
sayakṣōragarākṣasam,
jagadvaśe vartatedaṁ
kṛṣṇasya sacarācaram. (15)

All this world, that which moves and moves not, and which has Devas, Rakshasas and Gandharvas, and also Asuras and Nagas, are under the control of Lord Krishna.

इन्द्रियाणि मनो बुद्धिः
सत्त्वं तेजो बलं धृतिः ।
वासुदेवात्मकान्याहुः
क्षेत्रं क्षेत्रज्ञ एव च ।।१६।।

indriyāṇi manō buddhiḥ
sattvaṁ tejō balaṁ dhṛtiḥ,
vāsudevātmakānyāhuḥ,
kṣetraṁ kṣetrajña eva ca. (16)

The senses, mind, intellect, Sattva, splendour, strength and patience are said to be composed of Vasudeva, the field and the knower of the field.

सर्वागमानामाचारः
प्रथमं परिकल्प्यते ।
आचारप्रभवो धर्मो
धर्मस्य प्रभुरच्युतः ।।१७।।

sarvāgamānāmācāraḥ
prathamaṁ parikalypate,
ācāraprabhavō dharmō
dharmasya prabhuracyutaḥ. (17)

The conduct of all the Vedas is first conceived as the origin of conduct, the Dharma, the Lord of Dharma, the infallible.

ऋषयः पितरो देवा
महाभूतानि धातवः ।
जङ्गमाजङ्गमं चेदं
जगन्नारायणोद्भवम् ।।१८।।

ṛṣayaḥ pitarō devā
mahābhūtāni dhātavaḥ,
jaṅgamājaṅgamaṁ cedaṁ
jagannārāyaṇōdbhavam. (18)

The sages, the forefathers, the gods, the great beings, the metals, the movable and the immovable, this universe is born of Narayana.

योगो ज्ञानं तथा साङ्ख्यं
विद्याः शिल्पादि कर्म च ।
वेदाः शास्त्राणि विज्ञानमेतत्सर्वं
जनार्दनात् ।।१९।।

yōgō jñānaṁ tathā sāṁkhyaṁ
vidyāḥ śilpādikarma ca,
vedāśśāstrāṇi vijñānametatsarvaṁ
janārdanāt. (19)

Yoga, knowledge and also Sankhya, the sciences, crafts and other actions, the Vedas, and the scriptures, all this comes from Janardana.

एको विष्णुर्महद्भूतं
पृथग्भूतान्यनेकशः ।
त्रींल्लोकान्व्याप्य भूतात्मा
भुङ्क्ते विश्वभुगव्ययः ॥२०॥

ekō viṣṇurmahadbhūtaṁ
pṛthagbhūtānyanekaśaḥ,
trīn–lōkānvyāpya bhūtātmā
bhuṅkte viśvabhugavyayaḥ. (20)

Vishnu alone, the Great Being, pervading the three worlds with many separate beings, the soul of beings, enjoys the expanse of the Enjoyer of the universe.

इमं स्तवं भगवतो
विष्णोर्व्यासेन कीर्तितम् ।
पठेद्य इच्छेत्पुरुषः
श्रेयः प्राप्तुं सुखानि च ।।२१।।

imaṁ stavaṁ bhagavatō
viṣṇōrvyāsena kīrtitam,
paṭhedya Icchetpuruṣaḥ
śreyaḥ prāptuṁ sukhāni ca. (21)

Any man who desires to attain prosperity and happiness should recite this hymn of Lord Vishnu recited by Vyasa.

विश्वेश्वरमजं देवं
जगतः प्रभुमव्ययम् ।
भजन्ति ये पुष्कराक्षं न
ते यान्ति पराभवम् ।।२२।।

न ते यान्ति पराभवम् ॐ नम इति ।

viśveśvaramajaṁ devaṁ
jagataḥ prabhavāpyayam,
bhajanti ye puṣkarākṣaṁ na
te yānti parābhavam. (22)

na te yānti parābhavam oṃ nama iti.

Those who worship the lotus-eyed Lord of the universe, the unborn God, the Lord of the universe, the inexhaustible, do not get defeated.

- अर्जुन उवाच -

पद्मपत्रविशालाक्ष
पद्मनाभ सुरोत्तम ।
भक्तानामनुरक्तानां त्राता
भव जनार्दन ।।२३।।

- arjuna uvāca -

padmapatraviśālākṣa
padmanābha surottama,
bhaktānāmanuraktānāṃ trātā
bhava janārdana. (23)

- Arjuna said -

O lotus-petalled, large-eyed, lotus-navelled, best of the gods, be the saviour of the devotees who are devoted to you, O Janardana.

- श्रीभगवानुवाच -

योमां नामसहस्रेण स्तोतुमिच्छति पाण्डव ।
सोहऽमेकेन श्लोकेन स्तुत एव न संशयः ।।२४।।

स्तुत एव न संशय ॐ नम इति ।

- śrī bhagavānuvāca -

yō māṁ nāmasahasrēṇa
stōtumicchati pāṁḍava,
sōhamēkēna ślōkēna stuta
ēva na saṁśayaḥ. (24)

stuta eva na saṃśaya oṃ nama iti

- The Lord said -

He who likes, Oh Arjuna, to sing my praise, using these thousand names, should know Arjuna, that I would be satisfied By his singing of even one stanza, without any doubt. Om Nama, without any doubt.

- व्यास उवाच -

वासनाद्वासुदेवस्य वासितं भुवनत्रयम् ।
सर्वभूतनिवासोऽसि वासुदेव नमोऽस्तु ते ।।२५।।

श्री वासुदेव नमोऽस्तुत ॐ नम इति ।

- vyāsa uvāca -

vāsanādvāsudēvasya
vāsitaṁ tē jagatrayam,
sarvabhūtanivāsōsi
vāsudēva namōstu tē. (25)

śrīvāsudēva namōstuta ōṁ nama iti.

- Vyasa said -

My salutations to you Vasudeva, because You who live in all the worlds make these worlds as places where beings live, and also Vasudeva, You live in all beings as their soul.

Om Nama Iti.

- पार्वत्युवाच -

केनोपायेन लघुना
विष्णोर्नामसहस्रकम् ।
पठ्यते पण्डितैर्नित्यं
श्रोतुमिच्छाम्यहं प्रभो ।।२६।।

- pārvatyuvāca -

kēnōpāyēna laghunā
viṣṇōrnāmasahasrakam,
paṭhyatē paṁḍitairnityaṁ
śrōtumicchāmyahaṁ prabhō. (26)

- Parvathi said -

I am desirous to know, Oh Lord, how the scholars of this world will chant without fail these thousand names, by a method that is easy and quick.

Chant this shloka three times

- ईश्वर उवाच -

श्रीराम राम रामेति रमे रामे मनोरमे ।
सहस्रनाम तत्तुल्यं राम नाम वरानने ।।२७।।

श्रीरामनाम वरानन ॐ नम इति ।

- īśvara uvāca -

rīrāma rāma rāmēti
ramē rāmē manōramē,
sahasranāmatattulyaṁ
rāmanāma varānanē. (27)

śrī rāmanāma varānana ōṁ nama iti.

- Lord Shiva said -

Chanting the name of Rama fulfills all desires. Speaking Rama's name once is equal to a thousand names.

- ब्रह्मोवाच -

नमोऽस्त्वनन्ताय सहस्रमूर्तये
सहस्रपादाक्षिशिरोरुबाहवे ।
सहस्रनाम्ने पुरुषाय शाश्वते
सहस्रकोटियुगधारिणे नमः ।।२८।।

सहस्रकोटियुगधारिणे ॐ नम इति ।

- brahmōvāca -

namōstvanaṁtāya sahasramūrtayē
sahasrapādākṣiśirōrubāhavē,
sahasranāmnē puruṣāya śāśvatē
sahasrakōṭiyugadhāriṇē namaḥ. (28)

sahasrakōṭiyugadhāriṇē nama ōṁ nama iti.

- Brahma said -

Salutations to Thee, Oh Lord, Who runs the immeasurable time of thousands of crore yugas, Who has no end, Who has a thousand names, Who has a thousand forms, Who has a thousand feet, Who has a thousand eyes, Who has a thousand heads, Who has a thousand arms, and Who is always there.

Om Nama He who runs
thousands of crore yugas.

– संजय उवाच –
यत्र योगेश्वरः कृष्णो
यत्र पार्थो धनुर्धरः ।
तत्र श्रीर्विजयो भूतिर्ध्रुवा
नीतिर्मतिर्मम ।।२६।।

- sanjaya uvāca -

yatra yōgēśvaraḥ kr̥ṣṇō
yatra pārthō dhanurdharaḥ,
tatra śrīrvijayō bhūtirdhruvā
nītirmatirmama. (29)

- Sanjaya said -

Where Krishna, the king of Yogas, and where the wielder of bow, Arjuna, are there, there will exist all the good, all the the victory, all the fame, and all the justice in this world.

– श्रीभगवानुवाच –

अनन्याश्चिन्तयन्तो
मां ये जनाः पर्युपासते ।
तेषां नित्याभियुक्तानां
योगक्षेमं वहाम्यहम् ।।३०।।

- śrībhagavānuvāca -

ananyāścimtayamtō
mām yē janāḥ paryupāsatē,
tēṣām nityābhiyuktānām
yōgakṣēmam vahāmyaham. (30)

- Shri Bhagavan said -

I would take care of worries and cares of him who thinks of Me and serves Me without any other thoughts.

परित्राणाय साधूनां
विनाशाय च दुष्कृताम् ।
धर्मसंस्थापनार्थाय
सम्भवामि युगे युगे ।।३१।।

paritrāṇāya sādhūnāṁ
vināśāya ca duṣkr̥tām,
dharmasaṁsthāpanārthāya
saṁbhavāmi yugē yugē. (31)

I save the righteous and destroy the wicked, and establish righteousness in every age.

आर्ताः विषण्णाः शिथिलाश्च भीताः
घोरेषु च व्याधिषु वर्तमानाः ।
सङ्कीर्त्य नारायणशब्दमात्रं
विमुक्तदुःखाः सुखिनो भवन्ति ।।३२।।

ārtā viṣaṇṇāḥ śithilāśca bhītāḥ
ghōrēṣu ca vyādhiṣu vartamānāḥ,
saṁkīrtya nārāyaṇaśabdamātraṁ
vimuktaduḥkhāḥ sukhinō bhavaṁti. (32)

If he who is worried, sad, broken, afraid, severely ill, if he who has heard tidings bad, sings Narayana Narayana, all his cares will be taken care of.

कायेन वाचा मनसेन्द्रियैर्वा
बुद्ध्यात्मना वा प्रकृतेः स्वभावात् ।
करोमि यद्यत् सकलं परस्मै
नारायणायेति समर्पयामि ।।३३।।

kāyena vācā manaseṃdriyairvā
budhyātmanā vā prakṛteḥ svabhāvāt,
karomi yadyat sakalaṃ parasmai
nārāyaṇāyeti samarpayāmi. (33)

Whatever I do by either body, speech, mind or sensory organs, with either my personal knowledge or natural trait, I surrender and submit all to that to Supreme Divine Narayana.

इति
श्रीविष्णोर्दिव्यसहस्रनामस्तोत्रं
सम्पूर्णम् ।
ॐ तत् सत् ।

iti
śrīviṣṇordivyasahasranāmastotraṃ
sampūrṇam.

oṃ tat sat.

This is the complete Divya Sahasranama Stotram of Shri Vishnu.

Om Tat Sat.

Auspicious Dates and Times for Vishnu Puja

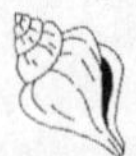

Satyanarayan Puja

'Satya' means 'truth' and Narayana means 'the highest being' so Satyanarayan means 'the highest being who is an embodiment of Truth'. The Satyanarayan Vrat and Puja are very popular all over India.

This puja is first mentioned in Skanda Purana, Reva Kanda, by Suta Puranik to the rishis in Naimisharanya. The details are part of the Katha (story) that is usually read along with the puja.

This puja is usually performed on the Purnima (full moon) day of every month. It is also performed on special occasions and during times of achievements as an offering of gratitude to the Lord. These occasions could include marriage graduation, start of a new job, and purchase of a new home, to name a few. In addition, the performance of this most auspicious puja generally confers a child to couples trying to start a family.

The Satyanarayan Puja can be performed on any day except on new moon. It is not a puja confined to any festivities, but Purnima is considered specifically auspicious for this puja. Performing this puja in the evening is considered more appropriate. However, one can perform this puja in the morning as well.

Benefits of Satyanarayan Puja

- Performing Satyanarayan Puja at home can bring in success. People who do this puja can achieve their goals and fulfil their aspirations.
- It can also improve physical and mental health of individuals drastically.
- It can help devotees enjoy a fulfilling material life and increases overall familial prosperity too.
- It can remove all sins from the past life.

Procedure of Satyanarayan Puja

The Satyanarayan Puja starts by offering a prayer to Lord Ganesha so that all obstacles that could probably occur if the puja is performed incorrectly is removed successfully. This can be achieved by chanting different names of Lord Ganesha and offering him

Prasada (food offered to the gods). Lord Ganesha is fond of Modak, which is a mixture of coconut and sugar, or he may be offered Laddoo. Showering the lord with flower petals is the final procedure.

Another important part of this prayer involves praying to the Navagraha or the nine significant celestial entities in this universe. They consist of the following names:

1. **Surya** - Sun
2. **Chandra** - Moon
3. **Angaraka** - Mars
4. **Buddha** - Mercury
5. **Brihaspati** - Jupiter
6. **Suka** - Venus
7. **Sani** - Saturn
8. **Rahu** - North Node, or the head of Svarbhanu
9. **Ketu** - South Node as the body with a tail of Svarbhanu

The remaining ritual consists of offering prayers and worshipping Satyanarayan, one of the most benevolent forms of Lord Vishnu. The first step is to clean the place where the deity is to be placed. Once the deity is placed in the correct position, Satyanarayan Swami can be worshipped. Names of Lord Satynarayana can be chanted along with various offerings like Prasada in the form of fruits, sweets, etc.

Another important requirement for this puja is the story of Satyanarayan, which is to be heard by all devotees taking part in this puja. This story entails the origin of the ritual, potential mishaps that could occur if any step is forgotten, and the benefits of this puja. Stories on Satyanarayan Vrat are provided in detail further on.

The prayer is concluded with Aarti, a ritual consisting of revolving a fire-lit lamp within close vicinity of Lord Satyanarayan's image. After the puja, all assembled join in on singing bhajans and chanting glories of the Lord. Finally, all present there are asked to partake of the Prasada that was offered to the Lord and seek Lord's blessings.

Bhadrapada Purnima

This full-moon day in the Bhadrapada month is considered a sacred time for worshipping Vishnu and the Moon deity. It is believed to be a powerful time to manifest goals, cleanse the mind, and make a fresh start.

Bhadrapada Purnima holds immense religious and

spiritual significance for Hindus. It is considered one of the most auspicious days for worshipping Lord Vishnu and the Moon deity. Falling on Purnima in the Bhadrapada month, this occasion is viewed as a sacred time for manifesting one's desires and goals. It also marks a powerful moment to release past emotions, cleanse the mind and heart, and make a fresh start on one's spiritual journey.

Bhadrapada Purnima Puja Rituals

- Take a holy bath in the morning.
- Make a Sankalp (vow) to observe the fast.
- Clean your home and altar for the puja.
- Place an idol of Lord Satyanarayan and offer Tulsi Patra (basil leaves), sweets and a yellow garland.
- Light a ghee diya and chant Lord Vishnu's mantras.
- Recite the Satyanarayan Vrat Katha before sunset.
- Prepare and offer Prasada (Panchamrit and Panjeeri) to the Lord.
- Sing Aarti ('Om Jai Jagdish Hare').
- Worship the moon and offer Kalash water.
- Distribute Prasad among attendees.

Dhanurmas

This month is considered especially auspicious for performing Vishnu puja. Some say that worshipping Vishnu on a single day during this period is equal to worshipping him for 1,000 years.

This period of month is considered as highly auspicious for Vishnu devotees. Old Hindu scriptures have set apart this month to be completely focused on devotional activities. Other non-devotional activities (such as weddings, purchase of property, etc.) arc prohibited during this month so that attention can be given exclusively to the worship of the God without any diversions. In South India, especially the Vaikunta Ekadasi, which falls during Dhanurmas, attracts thousands of devotees. Temples conduct special pujas during this period.

Shri Krishna in the Bhagavad Gita (10.35), says 'मासानां मार्गशीर्षोहम् (I manifest more in Margashirsha Mas among the different months in a year).'

According to tradition, the gods wake up early in the morning during Dhanurmas. They perform special prayers to Shri Maha Vishnu during the auspicious period of 'Brahm Muhurta', which is one and a half hours before sunrise. During this month, devotees offer prayers to the Lord very early in the morning. The month of Dhanurmas is considered a very special month for performing Vishnu Puja.

Dhanurmas Phal Shruti: Worshipping Vishnu on a single day during this auspicious period is equal to worshipping Vishnu with devotion for 1,000 years. Every single step taken towards the nearby lake, river, etc. for morning dip during this month brings forth merit equal to performing Ashvamedha Yajna.

During this period, the sun is in the Sagittarius or धनु राशि, the period when the sun passes from Sagittarius to Capricorn or मकर राशि is considered as a period of scarcity to the plenty in India. Feeding or giving alms to the deserving poor and Brahmins during this period is believed to confer great merit, i.e., Punya.

Vishnu Puja: Vidhi and Benefits

Lord Vishnu is one of the principal deities of Hinduism, worshipped as the preserver and protector of the universe. His worship is prevalent throughout India. Moreover, He is one of the most important deities in Hinduism. Vishnu Puja Vidhi is a set of rituals and prayers performed to worship Lord Vishnu. Here we have various aspects of this puja, including the mantras and their benefits.

Why Should One Perform Vishnu Puja?

According to astrology, performing Vishnu Puja can bring numerous benefits to individuals, including spiritual, emotional and physical well-being.

Vishnu is the preserver of the universe and the sustainer of life. According to astrology, performing Vishnu Puja can bring peace, prosperity and harmony to the life of a native. It can also help individuals overcome difficulties and obstacles in their lives and help them achieve success and prosperity.

Moreover, Lord Vishnu is the God of love, compassion and kindness. Performing His puja can help individuals develop these qualities and foster healthy relationships with their loved ones. It can also help individuals overcome negative emotions like anger and jealousy. Moreover, it can promote a positive outlook on life.

Also, Vishnu Puja has healing properties that can help individuals recover from physical ailments and promote overall health and well-being. According to astrology, performing this puja can help individuals overcome mental-health issues like anxiety, depression and stress.

Additionally, it is a powerful tool for spiritual growth and enlightenment. It can help individuals connect with their inner selves and develop a deeper understanding of their purpose in life. It can also help individuals overcome negative karma and achieve spiritual liberation.

Performing this puja can bring numerous benefits to individuals, including spiritual, emotional and physical well-being. It can help individuals overcome difficulties and obstacles and achieve success and prosperity. It can also help individuals develop positive qualities like love, compassion and kindness, and foster healthy relationships with their loved ones.

What Are the Preparations Needed for the Puja?

Before starting the puja, the devotee must prepare themselves and the place of worship. Here are the steps to prepare for the puja:

- ***Clean the place of worship:*** The place of worship should be cleaned thoroughly before the puja. It includes cleaning the floor, walls and area around the deity.
- ***Decorate the place of worship:*** Decorate the worshipping place with flowers, rangolis and other items.
- ***Arrange the puja items:*** The devotee must arrange all the items required for the puja, including the idol of Lord Vishnu, flowers, fruits, incense sticks, lamps and other items.
- ***Take a bath:*** The devotee must bathe before starting the puja to purify themselves.

How to Perform the Vishnu Puja?

Follow these steps to perform the Vishnu Puja and seek the maximum benefits of Lord Vishnu:

- The puja must begin with a prayer to Lord Ganesha for obstacle removal.
- Devotees must offer water to Lord Vishnu for His bath.
- Moreover, devotees must offer flowers and fruits to Lord Vishnu. Devotees must light a lamp and offer it to Lord Vishnu.
- Also, recite Vishnu mantras during the puja. These mantras are powerful and have several benefits.
- Ahead, offer food to Lord Vishnu and conclude the puja by performing the Aarti of Lord Vishnu.

Mantras to Chant During Vishnu Puja

Here are some of the mantras you can recite during Vishnu Puja:

- ***Om Namo Bhagavate Vasudevaya:*** This mantra is one of the most important mantras for Lord Vishnu. Chant it to seek the blessings of Lord Vishnu and purify the mind and body.
- ***Shri Vishnu Sahasranama:*** This mantra is a collection of 1,000 names of Lord Vishnu. Chanting

this mantra can bring peace, prosperity and good health.

- ***Shri Vishnu Gayatri Mantra:*** This mantra is to seek the blessings of Lord Vishnu. Reciting it can help overcome obstacles and bring success.

How Can Performing Vishnu Puja Help You?

Performing puja of Lord Vishnu is a sacred Hindu ritual that involves the worship of Lord Vishnu, one of the principal deities in Hinduism. According to astrology, performing Vishnu Puja can bring numerous benefits to individuals. Here are 11 benefits of performing Vishnu Puja as per astrology:

- Performing this puja can help individuals seek the protection of Lord Vishnu and overcome negative energies and obstacles in their lives.
- The puja of Lord Vishnu can help individuals seek the blessings of Lord Vishnu and attain prosperity and success in their lives.
- Vishnu Puja has healing properties. Moreover, it can help individuals overcome physical ailments and promote overall health and well-being.
- Performing Vishnu Puja can help individuals seek the blessings of Lord Vishnu and recover from illnesses.

- Also, Vishnu Puja can help individuals develop inner peace and tranquility and overcome negative emotions like anger and anxiety.
- This puja can help people develop these qualities and foster healthy relationships with their loved ones.
- It can help individuals connect with their inner selves and develop a deeper understanding of their purpose in life.
- Performing Puja of Lord Vishnu can help individuals overcome negative karma and attain spiritual liberation.
- Also, this puja can help individuals seek the blessings of Lord Vishnu and attain harmony and balance in their lives.
- Performing Vishnu Puja can help individuals seek the blessings of Lord Vishnu and overcome difficulties in their lives.
- Lastly, performing Vishnu pujan can help individuals attain mental peace and tranquility, and overcome negative emotions like stress and anxiety.

Benefits of Chanting Vishnu Mantras

Chanting Vishnu mantras has several benefits. Here are some of the benefits of chanting Vishnu mantras:

- Chanting Vishnu mantras can help purify the mind and body
- Reciting it can help remove obstacles from one's life and bring success.
- Chanting any of these mantras can protect against negative energies and evil forces.
- Moreover, chanting Vishnu mantras can bring peace and calmness to the mind and help reduce stress and anxiety.
- Chanting Vishnu mantras can improve physical and mental health and help prevent diseases.
- Also, Vishnu mantras can help one connect with the divine and increase spiritual growth.
- Chanting Vishnu mantras with devotion and sincerity can help fulfill one's wishes and desires.